BOOKS BY WILLO DAVIS ROBERTS

The View From the Cherry Tree
Don't Hurt Laurie!
The Minden Curse
More Minden Curses

More

MINDEN
CURSES

More

MINDEN
CURSES

by

Willo Davis Roberts

ILLUSTRATED BY SHERRY STREETER

Atheneum · *New York*

1980

LIBRARY OF CONGRESS CATALOGING IN PUBLICATION DATA

Roberts, Willo Davis.
More Minden curses.

Sequel to The Minden curse.
SUMMARY: When the Minden Curse involves Danny with
the old Caspitorian house, he discovers the secret
of its hauntedness and lost treasure and
helps foil a schemer who wants both
the house and treasure.
[1. Mystery and detective stories. 2. Buried
treasure—Fiction] I. Streeter, Sherry. II. Title.
PZ7.R54465Mo   79-22670
ISBN 0-689-30759-4

Text copyright © 1980 by Willo Davis Roberts
Illustrations © 1980 by Sherry Streeter
All rights reserved
Published simultaneously in Canada by
McClelland & Stewart, Ltd.
Manufactured by The American Book — Stratford Press, Inc.
Saddle Brook, New Jersey
Designed by M. M. Ahern
First Edition

More
MINDEN
CURSES

1

School started two weeks late in Indian Lake that fall. It wasn't late enough for me. I never wanted to go in the first place, any more than I wanted to stay behind with Aunt Mattie and Gramps Minden when my dad went off to take pictures in Ireland for *On the Spot Magazine*.

Gramps turned out to be pretty neat, for an old man, and there was the bonus of having Leroy for a dog, even if he did get me into quite a bit of trouble. But I didn't look forward to going to that goldanged old school. Goldanged is one of Gramp's swear words, and even I can say it in front of Aunt Mattie without making her eyebrows go up.

Actually, living in Indian Lake hadn't been as bad as I'd expected. With Leroy's help I'd gotten involved in all kinds of adventures, including a mystery, and after I got over being scared half to death, it was interesting to write to my dad about it.

The day school started, though, I figured the mysteries were all over—after all, how many mysteries can you have in a town with only about two thousand people?—and from then on it was going to be just boring, boring, boring.

If it hadn't been for the Minden Curse, I don't suppose I'd have found another mystery. There were quite a few kids in town who had lived there all their lives, and *they* didn't get involved with the Cat Ladies.

Aunt Mattie's mouth goes flat and tight whenever anything happens that she thinks is caused by the Minden Curse. I only found out about it when I came to stay with her and Gramps, but Gramps says Leroy and I have it, too. I guess we do, or I wouldn't have been mixed up in so many weird things from the time I got there.

It isn't really a curse, exactly. It just seems to work out that those who have it are always around when anything interesting happens. Like when the bank is robbed, or the mayor's wife falls off the ladder at the church and breaks her leg, or when there's a kidnapping. That kind of thing. The sheriff said he'd never seen such a crime wave as there was after I came to Indian Lake and had the curse, too.

Anyway, it didn't occur to me that the curse was

working when I set out for school that first morning. It was just plain life. I got up and had pancakes and sausages for breakfast. Aunt Mattie makes good pancakes. That morning I wished I hadn't had them though; they felt like a brick sitting in my stomach. Heavy, even though the pancakes themselves were as light and fluffy as they always were.

"You're not nervous about going to school for the first time, are you, Danny?" Aunt Mattie asked when I was ready to go out the door.

Why do grown-ups ask such stupid questions? How else could I be, but nervous? Even C.B. Hope was nervous about going to a new school, and she'd been going to schools all her life.

I knew better than to admit it, though. Aunt Mattie means well, but as Gramps says, she gets carried away sometimes. She'd have told me all the reasons why I didn't have anything to be nervous about. So I just said, "No, of course not," and took my lunch sack and my new notebook and went out the back door.

The back door faces the road, at our house. That's because all the houses along the lake have their front doors facing the lake. Leroy was sitting on the steps, that fool way he does, as if he's a person, with his rump on the top step and his front feet a couple of steps down. He got up, wagging his tail, sniffing my roast beef sandwiches through the paper bag.

"No," I told him. "You can't go this time. You'll have to stay."

Leroy looked at me, and his tail almost stopped wagging. Leroy is part Irish wolfhound, and he's one of the biggest and homeliest dogs I've ever seen. He's smart, though. He's rescued little kids from fires and drownings and outwitted some kidnappers.

"Stay," I said.

His tail drooped. In fact, Leroy drooped all over.

"I'll be home this afternoon," I said. "So you just stay, right?"

You never saw a sadder looking dog. But he stayed there on the porch as I went down the steps and onto the road.

I could see C.B. Hope walking up ahead of me. I could have yelled at her to wait and we'd walk together. Something told me maybe, at least that first day, we'd be better off if we didn't arrive together.

C.B.'s real name is Clarissa Beatrix, only she doesn't like it if anybody calls her that. She had always gone to a big fancy school in the city, but this year her family was staying in Indian Lake, so she was starting at a new school, too.

There was a school bus to pick up the kids who lived more than two miles from school. That didn't cover C.B. and me; we had to walk. I wondered what it would be like in the winter when there was snow on the ground.

I must have been over half a mile along the road, going past all the cottages and houses that were closed up until next summer, when intuition made me turn and look back. Intuition is that funny little thing inside of you that tells you something without your ever knowing why you know it.

And there, in the middle of the road, was Leroy. He stopped the minute I turned around, dropping his head in a guilty way. The end of his tail wagged, just once, and then he waited.

I glared at him. "Go home! Go on, go home!"

Leroy wilted, like a lettuce leaf when you accidentally run hot water on it instead of cold. He didn't move, though, except to sink closer to the ground.

"Go home, Leroy! I'm going to school, and they don't allow dogs at school!"

He tried to press himself into the gravel and pretend he didn't hear me.

I didn't know much about schools, never having been to one before, but I was pretty sure they wouldn't allow a dog there, especially not one the size of a Shetland pony.

I didn't have a watch, so I couldn't tell how much time I had. I'd left early, though, so maybe there was time to take him back, if I ran.

"OK, come on," I told him, and started to jog back toward the house. Leroy leaped up then, with his tongue hanging out and his ears flying back in the wind. It was all a big game to Leroy.

Aunt Mattie came out onto the porch when we trotted into the yard. "What's the matter? What did you forget?"

"Nothing. Only Leroy followed me. I guess I'll have to tie him up," I said.

She told me where to find a length of clothesline, and I knotted it through his collar and left him fastened to one of the clothesline posts. He looked so forlorn I almost felt sorry for him, except that now I had to hurry, if I expected to get to school on time.

I slowed down to a walk when I got to the edge of town. I could see a few other kids walking in the same direction, so I figured I must have enough time left. I decided I'd better take the shortest way, though.

I passed the sheriff's office, with the fire hydrant in front of it that Mrs. Trentwood had driven over, and Ben Newton was there, in his tan uniform with the badge on his pocket. He waved, and I waved back.

Then I cut through on the street that went past the Community Church, where Aunt Mattie sang in the choir every Sunday, and over past the house where Paul Engstrom lived, toward the school. I was alongside an old house set back in some trees when I realized two things: there was a great big black cat sitting atop the gate post at the front of that old house, and Leroy had sneaked up behind me.

Actually, I wouldn't have known the dadratted (that's another one of Gramp's swear words) dog was there except for the look of that cat.

He was huge already, but when he started to swell up, the way cats do when they're threatened by dogs, he was enormous. Even if it was just his hair standing on end, it was enough to make mine do it, too.

He sat there on the post, with a fancy collar around his neck, looking down with amber-colored eyes that were mean as mean can get. His hair stood out, and he spat.

Naturally, since I was almost alongside him, I jumped back and nearly trampled on Leroy. He had the grace to look mildly ashamed, and he was trailing a bit of clothesline around his neck where he'd chewed himself loose. Before I could even say anything, though, Leroy forgot he was in disgrace and made a lunge at that cat.

When Leroy sits down, his head is almost high enough for him to lick me in the face. And when he stands on his hind legs, he can easily look over a six-foot fence.

The gatepost wasn't anywhere near six feet tall.

Leroy went after the cat just about the time I got my wits together and grabbed for the trailing rope. I hauled him off just before he got his face scratched, because that big black cat wasn't giving an inch; as it was, he made a swipe with one white-tipped paw that couldn't have missed Leroy's nose by a quarter of an inch.

"Stop it, you fool dog!" I yelled, hauling back on the rope. "It would serve you right if I let him scratch you! Maybe you'd learn something! Sit!"

Leroy sat, grinning at me in that way he has when he's having fun, with his tongue lolling out.

The cat made a leap for the lower branches of a big oak tree and from that point of safety looked down at us with the most malevolent eyes I had ever seen. He looked really mean.

Leroy looked back, accepting defeat as gracefully as he did everything else, and thumped his tail on the sidewalk.

"What am I going to do with you now, you dumb old dog?" I felt like kicking him. I didn't because there was a lady on the porch of the huge old house watching us. "If I take you home again, I'll be late for school. Maybe you've made me late already. And if you go along to school, you'll just cause trouble."

Leroy's tail wagged a bit slower, though he was still grinning at me. There was enough rope left attached to his collar so he could be tied up again, maybe to a tree near the school grounds, only what would be the use? He'd just chew through it again.

I took off what was left of the rope and stuck it in my pocket. "OK. You're on your own. I'm going to pretend I don't know you," I said and took off walking as fast as I could.

Even so, I was late. The confounded bell was ringing as I went through the front doors. (I learned a lot of words from Gramps.) The hall was empty except for a statue of an Indian chief right in the middle of the front end of it.

I swallowed hard. I wasn't even sure where to go. Paul Engstrom had said he'd meet me inside the front doors, but I guessed he hadn't been able to wait.

A man came out of a door and looked toward me. He was a smallish man with thinning hair and he wore glasses. "You're a little late," he said mildly.

I guessed maybe he was Mr. Pepper, the principal.

"Yes, sir. My dog followed me, and I had to take him back home."

"Oh, yes. Leroy," he said, and then I *knew* he was Mr. Pepper. Leroy had rescued his little kids when one of them set a fire in the Pepper kitchen. "Well, let's see. You're going into the seventh grade, isn't that right?"

"Yes, sir," I said, and those pancakes now felt like *two* bricks in my stomach.

He took me along to a classroom and opened the door. There was a teacher at the front of the room, a little dried-up lady with gray hair. She turned and looked at us, and so did all the kids in the room.

"Miss Twitten, this is Danny Minden. He's going to be in your class this year," Mr. Pepper said.

"Well, come in and sit down," Miss Twitten said. She didn't sound particularly pleased to meet me.

"There's an empty seat right there in the front row."

I guessed Paul was in there, somewhere. I didn't have a chance to look. I felt very strange with all those faces turned in my direction, and I slid into the seat she'd indicated.

"I will expect everyone," she said, looking right at me, "to arrive for class *on time*."

My ears felt so hot I figured they were about as red as my hair.

After the first couple of minutes, though, it wasn't so bad. She was making up a list of our names and assigning seats. I felt a little better when she put me in one about halfway back, on the outside row. She had a yardstick she carried around all the time, to point at things, and sometimes she smacked someone over the knuckles with it. Although she didn't do it that first day, I kept expecting her to hit me.

"Hey, Danny!" A hoarse whisper drifted across the aisle. "What happened to you?"

"There will be no *talking* while I assign the seating," Miss Twitten said, so I didn't dare answer. I was glad that Paul was sitting right across the aisle from me, though. Paul was the only local kid I'd met so far, beside C.B. Hope, who wasn't really local. We hadn't started out too well together, but after we got acquainted we liked each other all right.

I didn't get to talk to him until recess. They didn't call it recess, they called it break time. We all went outside, and some of the kids went racing for balls and bats and stuff. When I stopped on the edge of the yard, Paul and three other kids came over right away.

"Hey, Danny, how come you were late?" Paul demanded. He was bigger than I was, being a year older, and so were the other guys. Because I'd studied with my dad, I was a year ahead in school for my age, which I didn't think was going to be an advantage.

"Leroy followed me. I took him back once, and then he caught up with me and tried to jump at a big black cat on a fence post. There was an old lady on the porch, so I didn't think it was a good idea to let him do it."

They all looked at each other as if I'd said something significant.

"Yeah? Where was this cat and the old lady? What did the house look like?" Paul asked.

"A great big house set back in the trees. Red, dark red color, with the paint sort of peeling on it. It has some towers or something, like an old wooden castle."

They all looked at each other again.

"Did Leroy tangle with Killer?" Paul asked.

"Who's Killer? The cat?"

"Big black devil with a white patch on his chest and two white front feet. Wears a red collar with jewels on it."

"Yeah, that's him. Is his name really Killer?"

"Well, I think the Cat Ladies call him Chester, but everybody else in town calls him Killer. There's not a dog in Indian Lake he hasn't licked."

"He hasn't licked Leroy. Not yet, anyway. Maybe it's a good thing I pulled him off when I did."

Paul licked his lips. "Did she say anything to you? The old lady?"

"No. Her cat was OK, he jumped up into a tree."

One of the other kids was about my height only a lot heavier. In fact, he was fat. "Did you see anything?" he asked.

"See anything? Anything like what?" I wanted to know.

"At the old house where the Cat Ladies live. Like a face in the upstairs window, or anything?"

"I didn't have time to look at the upstairs window. Why? What should I have seen?"

"Tubby saw a face there once, in one of the towers," Paul said. "That's Tubby Zazorian, you know; his dad is the manager of the bank."

I'd met Mr. Zazorian. I was in his bank when it got robbed, and Leroy and I recovered the money. We didn't get a reward, but we got our pictures in the paper.

"The house is haunted," Tubby said. I could see why they called him Tubby. He sure didn't look as if he missed very many meals.

I looked around at the other faces, wondering if they were putting me on. Come to think of it, the house looked like the kind that *would* be haunted.

"I didn't see anything," I said. "Who haunts it? Doesn't the old lady who lives there object?"

The biggest of the other kids scowled. "You think it's funny, do you? Are you making fun of our town?"

"No, hey, Frankie," Paul protested. "He just didn't know. Everybody calls them the Cat Ladies, because of all the cats they have. Their real names are Rosie and Anna Caspitorian. That's such a mouthful nobody ever calls them that. It's true, that house has some strange things happening there."

"Oh? Like what?" I tried not to sound skeptical, because that Frankie looked as if he were ready to use any excuse to get annoyed with me.

"Like lights and faces in the upper part of the house," Tubby said.

"Well, if there are two women who live there, why wouldn't they be in the upper part of the house sometimes?" I asked.

"They're old ladies," the third kid said. He was taller and skinnier than the others, and he wore glasses. He didn't look sissy or anything like that, though. He had a T-shirt on that showed pretty good muscles. "Miss Anna is in a wheelchair, and Miss Rosie has heart trouble so she can't climb the stairs. So if you ever see a face above the first floor, it's not one of them."

Paul jerked a thumb at the tall skinny kid. "This is

my friend Steve Baker. And he's Frankie Sloan. They've all been waiting to meet you, Danny."

Tubby and Steve looked friendly enough. Frankie didn't exactly give me the impression that he was dying to become my best friend. I nodded and said I was glad to meet all of them.

"Come on," Frankie said, "let's get a ball game going. We got time for about two innings."

I know it's only an expression when they say your heart sinks, but that was really what it felt like. My heart was way down in my stomach instead of where it belonged. It felt worse than the bricks that had been there after breakfast.

I'd only been in school a few hours and already I was going to have to display my ignorance.

"You want to play first base?" Steve asked me.

I was cold all over. "I don't know. I never played baseball before."

They all looked at me as if I'd suddenly sprouted a second head, except Paul. He knew already that I was no athlete except for swimming.

"You don't get a chance to play ball when you're traveling all the time, living in hotels," I said. It sounded lame, even to me.

"Well, maybe you better start out in right field, then," Steve said.

So we went out onto the field. There were some older kids having football practice in the next field over. High school kids, Paul said. "They don't let you play football until you're in the ninth grade here. But who cares? Baseball is more fun, anyway. Here, you can use my glove, Danny. I'll borrow one of the school's."

So I stood out there in the right field and sort of half prayed nobody would hit a ball in my direction, and half prayed that if they did, I'd be able to catch it.

I guess nobody up there was listening that day. A little skinny kid hit the ball right over my head, first thing. I jumped up and tried, knowing I'd never catch it, and I didn't. The ball sailed off across the grass, and even before I got up off my back, I heard the guys yelling. All of them, on both teams.

"Hey, bring it back!"

Wouldn't you know. It was Leroy. He had the ball and was galloping around the bases with it.

Tubby started to laugh. "Hey, a dog that plays baseball!"

Frankie didn't think it was funny, though, and I was already beginning to see that a lot of the kids took their cue from Frankie. If he laughed, they all did. If he scowled, they all waited to see what he was going to do.

For the second time that morning, my face and ears turned red. "Come on, give it here," I said. Leroy trotted over and dropped the ball into my hand, and

I threw it to Steve on the pitcher's mound.

"Guess you need a dog to catch the ball, if you can't do it yourself," Frankie said. "Come on, get that animal out of here, and let's play ball."

I was glad I'd saved the rope. I put it back on Leroy and tied him to a corner of the fence. I felt like kicking him that time, too.

Nobody hit a ball in my direction again, and the bell rang before I came up to bat. I decided I'd ask Paul, and maybe Steve, if they would get together with me after school some time and teach me to catch and hit without quite such a big audience. Particularly one that included Frankie Sloan.

The rest of the morning went pretty well up until lunchtime. I was writing out the assignment Miss Twitten had on the board when I heard people starting to shift in their seats and giggle.

"Danny Minden," Miss Twitten said in such a sharp, severe voice that I jerked in surprise and looked up.

"Is that your dog?" she demanded.

She knew it was. After Leroy found the money that was stolen from the bank and got his picture in the paper, everybody in town knew Leroy was my dog.

And there he was, poking his head in the doorway, with his tongue hanging out. When he saw me, he trotted over and began smelling around the desk for those roast beef sandwiches. The kids started laughing out loud, but the teacher didn't think it was amusing.

"Get him out of here," she said, articulating every syllable very carefully.

"Yes, ma'am," I agreed and sprang up to do it, knocking my notebook off the desk so that it skidded across the floor. When I bent over to pick it up, Leroy licked at my cheek, and I cracked my head on Paul's desk before I got everything sorted out. By now the kids were practically howling with delight. I wanted to sink through the floor.

I got that fool dog out in the hall, all right, and then I wondered what to do with him. I'd left him tied to the school yard fence and he'd chewed himself free a second time; there wasn't enough left of the clothesline to tie him anywhere again, even if there'd been any sense to it.

Mr. Pepper came along the hallway, carrying some papers. He stopped and smiled. "Well, having trouble, are you?"

"Yes, sir. He followed me into the classroom, and Miss Twitten told me to get rid of him. I guess he knows it's almost lunchtime, and I brought roast beef sandwiches."

"Ummm." He considered Leroy, who was wagging his tail. "Well, he's been entertaining the kindergarteners for the past hour. But I think he might have a disruptive influence on the other classes. And you won't have time to take him home during noon hour. I'll tell you what. Run over to the hardware store—your grandfather has a charge account there—and get a length of chain. A regular dog leash, maybe. And secure him with that. I'll explain to Miss Twitten."

So that's what I did.

I had to take Leroy with me, of course. And I took the shortest way to the hardware store, which led us back past that big old red house that looked like a wooden castle.

I took a better look at it this time, hanging onto Leroy's collar just in case that cat was still around, and saw that there were two round towers and a square one, besides all kinds of fancy decorations. Gingerbread, Aunt Mattie says they call it. It's really wood cut into the shape of scrolls and flowers and fancy designs.

And then I saw it and stumbled and fell over Leroy and scraped my knee on the sidewalk because I forgot to look where I was going.

And when I looked up again, it was still there.

A face at one of the tower windows, looking right down at me.

2

It was a warm day, but I felt like a breeze had blown over me right off the lake.

Had those kids been putting me on, or was it really peculiar that there was someone upstairs, on the third floor of the tower?

While I was looking at it, trying to decide if it was male or female, the face moved away and the curtains fell back into place.

Well, I couldn't stand there staring all day. I went on to the hardware store and told the man my problem, and he gave me the leash made out of chain he thought was strong enough to hold Leroy. I went back past the old red house and didn't see anything unusual that time. I fastened Leroy to a fencepost again and went into the school building just as the bell rang for noon. That was about the only good thing that happened all day, that I didn't have to walk back into that classroom and make a spectacle of myself again.

Everybody came boiling out of the room carrying their lunches. A few kids, mostly girls, had lunch pails. The rest of them had sacks, the same as I did.

"You want to eat with us?" Tubby asked. He had a bigger sack than anybody. When he opened it up and spread it out on a napkin on the ground, I couldn't believe it.

We sat on the grass near where Leroy was chained. There was a lunchroom, they told me, but nobody used it when the weather was good. We were allowed to eat outside as long as we picked up all our trash.

I was really hungry. I could have eaten all my lunch by myself, only it was impossible with Leroy sitting there drooling. That's what he did when he watched you eat; he'd let the saliva dribble out of the sides of his mouth and sort of grin at you, his eyes following every bite you took, until you gave in and shared with him.

Tubby traded me one of his candy bars for one of Aunt Mattie's oatmeal cookies. He gave Leroy half of a peanut butter sandwich, and I gave him half of one of my roast beef ones, and another kid I didn't know offered him a deviled egg. Naturally Leroy swallowed it whole.

"Come on," Frankie said, stuffing his wrappings back into the paper bag before I'd even started on my last cookie. "Let's get a ball game going."

On lunch hour, too? Was that all they did, play ball? I could have refused, of course, only where would that leave me in the business of getting to know my peers, as my dad was always saying I should do?

I bit off half the cookie and tossed the rest of it toward Leroy; he caught it before it hit the ground.

"I did see something this time when I went past that red house," I said. Anything to delay getting out there and making a fool of myself again. "There was somebody in one of the towers."

They all stopped and looked at me. "Who was it?" Paul asked. "Could you see?"

"Not very well. Just a face."

"We told you," Paul said, nodding. "Boy, that's a spooky place."

"Come on," Frankie said crossly. "Let's play ball."

So I had another session, and this time it was long enough so I came to bat, twice. Naturally, I struck out both times. At least nobody said anything about it, not that I heard, anyway.

The afternoon session was a little better. We went into Mr. Fowler's room for math. Math isn't my strong subject. Mr. Fowler seemed like a good teacher, though. He explained things so I knew what was going on. I already knew Mr. Fowler, of course. He and his wife had a little cottage out beyond our place.

He called on me to work out a problem. It was the first time I'd ever recited in front of a class, and I felt so hot I knew my ears were lighting up again. That happens to me when I'm embarrassed, and there's nothing I can do about it. It never bothered me to recite to my dad, but it was different standing up with a whole roomful of kids staring at me. At least I got the answer right.

After math we had music, and that was OK. And then we went back to our homeroom for English. I always did pretty well with that, so it didn't bother me even with Miss Twitten for a teacher. By that time I knew the kids referred to her as *Miss Twit*; they all made fun of her behind her back, but I noticed nobody got smart with her to her face. Not while she had that yardstick around.

As soon as school was out, Paul asked if I wanted to stick around and play ball for a few hours.

"Well, I'd like to," I said untruthfully. "Only Aunt Mattie thinks I'm coming straight home, and you know how she is. And I better get Leroy home, too. He's been on that short chain for a long time. Tell you what, Paul. Could we get together, with Steve, maybe, so you could give me some pointers about playing baseball? I've watched lots of it on

TV, but that's different from doing it yourself."

"Sure. And tell your aunt you'll be staying after school from now on, why don't you? So she won't expect you home?"

"OK," I agreed. For just a minute I almost hated my dad for going off and leaving me here like this.

I guess I was the only seventh grade boy who didn't stay to play ball. I unfastened Leroy from the fence, letting him lick my face a few times to show how happy he was that I'd finally come for him, and we started off home.

C.B. Hope caught up with us when we were about even with the old red house.

"Hi," she said. She was wearing a dress, the first time I had ever seen her in anything except jeans or shorts. Her hair was still straight and dark and came just below her ears and her eyes were still green, but she looked so different I felt uncomfortable. "I guess you survived the first day."

"Just barely," I said, and told her about it.

She didn't laugh. "Me, too," she said. She looked back over her shoulder at the wooden castle house. "I've heard about it, about the ones they call the Cat Ladies. I guess they have a houseful of cats. Everybody thinks they're—well, peculiar."

"Sometimes I think everybody's peculiar," I told her. "Except you and me, maybe."

C.B. grinned and suddenly she was familiar again.

25

Then she stopped grinning and walking and looked upward into the trees. There were big oaks in the front yard of the red house, and some of the branches stuck out over the sidewalk. "Listen."

I heard it, too, and so did Leroy. He whined, looking up through the leaves.

"It's a cat," I said.

"More like a kitten. It's such a tiny mewing sound." C.B. twisted her head. "Probably a dog chased it, and it got up into the tree and can't get down."

"Well, at least this time it wasn't Leroy." I would have gone on past, but C.B. has a soft spot for cats. She has one named Marcella.

"We'd better get it down, Danny."

"And how do you suggest that we do that?" I knew who she meant by *we*. She meant *me*.

"I can't climb a tree in a dress," she pointed out.

So, naturally, I climbed the tree and crawled out on a limb and rescued the kitten. It was little and white and fluffy and it had on a pale blue collar with glittery rhinestones all the way around it. It wouldn't come to me, just sat there crying, until I scrooched all the way out to it. The limb bent under my weight a little, but I got the kitten and handed it down to C.B.

"Isn't it cute? Look at the fancy collar! Oh, Danny, you've torn your pants!"

I slid down and stared at the three-cornered tear

in one knee. It was right over the place I'd skinned earlier, and the scab had been knocked off so it was bleeding again. At least they weren't new pants. Though I had a notion Aunt Mattie would purse her lips when she saw them.

Leroy was trying to get his nose on the kitten. He didn't want to hurt it, he only wanted to smell it, so C.B. held it down for him to touch. It was such a young kitten it didn't have sense enough to object; it just sat there, huddled in C.B.'s hands, while Leroy checked it over.

"We'd better take it back to the house," C.B. suggested.

Sometimes that girl really got some crazy ideas. "Why can't we dump it over the fence and let it go back on its own?" I wanted to know.

"It's so little, it may not find its way back. Probably a dog chased it, and now it's lost. It's such a *little* kitten, Danny."

So we fastened Leroy to the fence—he was getting so used to it now, he hardly even whined when we left him—and we went through the gate and up the path to the house.

The kids were right. The closer we got to that red house, the spookier it seemed. It was surrounded by trees, so it was mostly in shadow. It wasn't until we got right to the foot of the front steps that we saw the cats. They were all over the place. On the steps, on the porch railing, two of them on low tree branches. I couldn't count them all.

"We can put it down right here," I said. "See, it'll have lots of company."

"It's very badly frightened," C.B. informed me. "Its poor little heart is beating so fast. I think we'd better hand it over to the ladies who own it."

I thought she was being silly, and I said so. She didn't pay any attention, though. She walked right up the steps and across the porch and rang the bell. It was one of those old-fashioned kind that you twist, and it only rings inside as long as you keep twisting it. C.B. twisted it until the door opened.

The lady that opened it was walking, so I guessed she must be Miss Rosie, since the other one was supposed to be in a wheelchair. She didn't look frightening, especially. Just an old lady in a blue dress that had been mended; it was clean, and so was she.

"Oh, my, you've rescued Roscoe," she said cheerfully. "Where was he? Up a tree again?" She didn't wait for us to answer. "He hasn't learned yet to get down, but oh, how he can climb!"

Roscoe? It didn't seem a suitable name for a small, white, fluffy kitten. Maybe they had so many cats they were running out of names for them. Besides the ones we'd already seen outside, a big old tabby was rubbing against Miss Rosie's ankles.

"Danny climbed the tree and got him," C.B. said,

offering over the kitten.

"Well, that was nice of you, young man." She smiled at me, and I couldn't see anything peculiar about her. "And you kept your big dog from getting at Chester this morning too, didn't you?"

"I don't think Leroy meant to hurt him," I said quickly. "He's just a curious dog."

"Come in, come in. You've both been most helpful. You deserve a reward. Come on in."

She stepped backward, letting the door swing wide open. I started to say, "No, thank you," but C.B. was already going inside. I tried to kick at her ankle; she saw it coming and dodged.

Well, shoot, I thought. If C.B. went in, I might as well go in, too. I figured the guys must have been putting me on, after all, about this being a haunted house.

Once I got inside, though, following Miss Rosie and C.B. back through the house, I wasn't so sure.

There was hardly any light. What there was showed faded wallpaper, peeling in some places. There were lace curtains at the windows; some of them had been darned, and some of them were simply falling to pieces. The furniture, in the rooms I could see into, was really old-fashioned. Plush sofas and chairs, all with those lacy things on the backs and arms.

Anyway, the boards creaked under our feet, and

when I looked up the stairs I thought for a minute there was somebody standing there. I nearly jumped a foot, and then I realized it was a mirror, reflecting the curtains blowing at a window on the landing. So much for ghosts.

It *was* spooky, though. Everything was so old, and the whole place had an odd smell, sort of musty. Something brushed against my leg, and I jerked before I looked down and saw it was another cat, a gray one.

We went all the way back through that enormous house. There were rooms on both sides of the hall, most of them with the shades drawn so everything looked gloomy and as if there might be someone hiding in the shadows.

We finally came out at the far end of the hall into a big kitchen. It smelled good out there, and we could see why. There were fresh cookies spread out on the table, and an old lady in a wheelchair, looking almost identical to Miss Rosie except that she wore a pink dress, was putting another panful into the oven of a big black wood-burning stove.

"We have company, Anna," Miss Rosie said loudly. "They rescued poor Roscoe. I do hope he learns to climb *down* pretty soon. I thought they might like some of your cooking as a reward."

Miss Anna nodded. "Help yourselves," she said, not smiling, and closed the oven door. Then she scooted around the table and moved her chair up to a sink and started doing the dishes she'd mixed the cookies in. I guess it was a special sink, because it was low enough for her to reach.

We each accepted a cookie. They were big thick ones, still warm, with chocolate chips and raisins and nuts in them. And while we chewed, C.B. talked to Miss Rosie and I counted cats.

There were fourteen of them in the kitchen. Every size and color you could think of.

After we'd each had three cookies, I said I thought it was time to go, and Miss Rosie gave me another cookie for my dog.

"I suppose he'll eat cookies," she said.

"He'll eat anything," I said, and then wondered if she'd think that included cats.

We were all the way to the front door when C.B. asked what I'd been wondering. "How many cats do you have?"

"Thirty-two," Miss Rosie said. "Or is it thirty-three? That big Siamese over there came last week, and he was either thirty-two or thirty-three, I forget. He looked so elegant, even though he was half-starved, that we're calling him the Prince of Wales. Prince, for short, of course."

He had a collar, too. In fact, they all did. All colors, all decorated with rhinestones or bits of colored glass. I wondered how come they kept buying fancy collars for their cats when they didn't fix the boards on their porch. I nearly fell through on the way out.

"Where do they all come from?" C.B. wanted to know, still talking about the cats.

"Oh, they seem to know, somehow, that we can be trusted to care for them," Miss Rosie said. "Every stray in the county finds us, sooner or later. We never turn one away."

Leroy was still where we'd left him, out in front. I let him loose and gave him the cookie—he swallowed it so fast he couldn't possibly have tasted it—and C.B. waved good-bye to Miss Rosie.

We started off toward home, and I didn't know whether to be mad at Paul and his friends or not. The sisters were ordinary old ladies, except for the number of cats they kept. As the new kid in town, I wondered how many more jokes I'd be made the butt of, before they decided I'd had enough.

And then, just before the house went out of sight behind the trees, I looked back and saw it again.

The face in the upstairs window. Before I could get C.B. to turn around and look, too, it was gone. There was only a ragged lace curtain to see.

And since we'd left the old sisters downstairs only a few minutes before, it certainly couldn't have been either Miss Rosie or Miss Anna. Not even I could have climbed to the top of the tower that fast. And they didn't climb at all.

I was kind of thoughtful walking home, after that.

3

At supper Aunt Mattie put me through a regular inquisition. Well, maybe not like the ones where they tortured people if they didn't give the right answers, but she sure wanted to know everything.

Which teachers did I get, and did I meet some nice kids, and how did I like it?

My dad says although it isn't a good thing to be a liar, sometimes it's good politics to refrain from telling the whole truth. I figured this was one of those times. I left out a lot. I saw Gramps looking at me across the platter of fried chicken, and I knew he suspected part of what I wasn't saying. When he winked at me, I was sure of it.

I worked the conversation around to the Caspitorian sisters, without actually saying I'd met them. I mentioned that C.B. and I had rescued one of their kittens and commented on what a big old house it was.

"Yes, it's the oldest house in town," Aunt Mattie said. "Anna and Rosie have lived in it all their lives; I think they were both born there, as a matter of fact."

"It's pretty fancy. Those towers and everything. Some of the kids at school said it's haunted."

Aunt Mattie got that expression on her face that she has when Gramps comes home from having been involved in another odd episode.

"I don't know where people get those ideas. The Caspitorians are just two old ladies who like to keep cats and don't care for much company. Neither of them hears very well, so I suppose making conversation isn't easy for them."

Maybe it meant they didn't hear anyone walking around up over their heads, either, I thought. Although it didn't seem likely anyone could be moving around up there without being seen, coming or going. They'd have to come down for something to eat, wouldn't they? At least, a live human would.

"It looks as if it cost a lot to build, even in the old days. It must have twenty rooms."

"Twenty-three, I think," Gramps said unexpectedly. "If you don't count the attic. Yes, it was a fancy place in the old days. Beginning to show its age, now. I noticed it needs a new roof; some of the shingles have blown off."

Aunt Mattie looked concerned. "I doubt if they

can afford to have anything done to it. Roofs cost the earth these days."

"Maybe if they didn't feed all those cats," I said, "they could afford a roof."

"That nephew of theirs could help them, if he wanted to," Aunt Mattie said, passing the potatoes and gravy around again. "But no, all he does is say they'd be better off in a rest home. Maybe they would be, in a way, but they couldn't take their cats with them. They're devoted to those cats."

"Well," Gramps said, leaning back and patting his stomach, "you can't help thinking it would be wonderful for them if the old stories were true. They could sure use that fortune, all right."

That perked me up, though I tried not to be too obvious about it. "What old stories, Gramps? What fortune?"

"Why, you mean those kids didn't tell you? That's supposed to be why the place is haunted."

"Dad!" Aunt Mattie said protestingly, "don't encourage him."

"Why not? It's a story everybody in Indian Lake knows, and Danny lives here now, he might as well hear it from me as from anybody else. Old man Caspitorian, that was their father, he was a rich man, owned the jewelry store, the one on Main Street. Had to be rich or he couldn't have built a house like that one. Rich and thrifty. He didn't waste any money on anything anybody else wanted, you see, only on things for himself. And he liked to keep track of what other people were doing. That was the reason for those towers. When the house was built, he could see all over the countryside from one or the other of 'em. When he got old and sick, about the age the girls are now, he insisted on staying in a bed up in one of those towers, so he could see what was going on. It made a lot of work for the people who took care of him, but he didn't care about that. Said that was what he paid 'em for."

"And he had a fortune? What happened to it, then? Why are his daughters so poor now?"

Aunt Mattie, disgusted that Gramps was indulging in gossip, as she called it, got up and went to get dessert. It was wild blackberry pie. I cut into mine and chewed slowly, so as to make it last longer. "What happened, Gramps?"

"Well, they say he was afraid someone would steal his money. Sometimes rich folks get that way, think people are trying to steal from them, whether it's true or not. I don't know if it was, in his case. I do know he had a lot of money, though, and that he didn't keep it in a bank. That was long before we had a bank here in Indian Lake, and he didn't trust banks, anyway. He lost some of what he had in the depression, and he wasn't going to let it happen again, so he kept it at home. In cash, they say. Anyway, he had it hid somewhere in the house. Then he got really sick, with a high fever for several days, went out of his head, everybody thought he was going to die, I guess. And when he came out of it, he couldn't remember where he'd put a dime of that money."

Gramps attacked his own pie with enthusiasm. You'd think, eating Aunt Mattie's cooking all those years, he'd have been fat instead of skinny.

"And nobody ever found it?" I asked incredulously. "Even after years and years?" It had to be a long time ago, if old Mr. Caspitorian was as old then as his daughters were now.

"If anybody did, they kept quite about it," Gramps said. "Sure as anything, Rosie and Anna never had any of it. It's all they can do to pay the taxes on the place, I reckon. Mattie, how about another piece of that pie? Just a sliver?"

So I had one, too, and we didn't talk about the Caspitorian sisters any more except for Gramps's summary: "So that's why people say the place is haunted. That the old man is still wandering around, trying to remember where he hid the money."

I let it go at that. But Paul said sometimes people saw someone moving around in the upper part of the old red wooden castle, and I'd seen somebody there today. Not once, but twice.

I didn't really think it was the ghost of old man Caspitorian.

I sure wondered who it was, though.

I hadn't wanted to mention in front of Aunt Mattie the problems I'd had with Leroy. She wasn't all that sold on having a big dog around to feed, and if he got into trouble I was afraid she'd decide we had to get rid of him.

I told Gramps, though, because I couldn't have Leroy following me to school every day.

"I guess we'll have to keep him chained," I said. That made me feel depressed, because Leroy loved his freedom. Even when I didn't go, he liked to run along the beach or through the woods.

"Well, maybe we don't have to be that drastic," Gramps said. "Tell you what. You shut him in the shed before you leave, and then after school starts I'll turn him loose. Chances are, he'll mosey around on his own until you come home."

That sounded better than having him tied up all day. So the next morning I saved half a sausage to entice Leroy into the shed and quick shut the door behind me.

Leroy barked and scratched at the door.

I tried to explain to him why he had to stay there for a while, and then I went on to school.

I almost made it on time that second morning, only not quite. Because when I was passing by the old Caspitorian house, watching for another face in the window, I got involved again. The Minden curse was working overtime.

It wasn't another face, though, it was smoke and somebody screaming.

I thought the house was on fire. The smoke was coming from the back, and I jumped over the fence and went running around the house. Miss Rosie was standing there beside an old oil barrel that had flames shooting up out of it. When I got up close, I could see that she'd singed the hair all around her face. She'd backed off before her hair really caught fire, but she'd burned her hands; I could tell by the way she was holding them.

I looked around, saw a hose coiled up in the grass, and followed it back to the faucet to turn on the water. In a few minutes I'd watered down the grass around the barrel and sprayed some against the side of the shed nearby, too.

"I think the rest of it will just burn itself out," I told her. "Are you hurt?"

"Just my hands, a little," Miss Rosie said. She looked scared, though she was calming down. "I don't know what happened; I put in some papers and when I lit them the way I always do, everything sort of exploded." She brushed a flake of ash off her dress front.

Already the flames were dying down, so I didn't put any water in the barrel. "It would be better if you didn't use gas or anything to start it burning," I said. "It's too dangerous."

"But I didn't!" She looked at me in astonishment. "I never put anything like that in the trash barrel!"

I didn't argue with her. I could smell it, though. Somebody had put gasoline in there, though I couldn't imagine why they would. Anyway, it was all under control now.

"I think if you put your hands in ice water, they'll feel better," I said. "Unless they're bad enough to go to the doctor." My dad did that for me once, when I had hot gravy spilled on my foot.

"I don't think so. My, I thank you for coming to help me," Miss Rosie said. "I was afraid the shed would catch fire, and it's so close to the house. An old wooden house like that, I don't suppose it would take much to burn it right to the ground."

"What's going on?" somebody said behind me, and we both turned around to see the man next door standing beside the fence. "Something wrong?"

"Oh, Mr. Holman. Yes, I had a little fire, but Danny's put it out. Do you know Danny Minden? Mr. Holman's our banker, Danny; he lives next door."

Mr. Holman was tall and skinny and had a lot of fuzzy hair except right in the middle, where he was bald. He looked at me as if he thought I'd started the fire, not put it out. "Wife said she heard you yell.

Glad everything's OK now." He turned away and went back to his own house, where his wife waited on the back porch. She was a little woman with carroty red hair, worse than mine, and lots of freckles.

"Well, if everything's OK, I'd better get on to school," I said. "I almost forgot where I was going."

So I took off, and I was only about two minutes late. I had to go to the office for a pass to get into Miss Twitten's class.

I thought Mr. Pepper would be annoyed, but he just smiled as he made out the pass. "This sort of thing going to happen to you every morning, Danny?" he asked.

"I hope not, sir," I told him.

Naturally, when I walked into the classroom, everybody turned to look at me. I had the pass Mr. Pepper had signed, so Miss Twitten didn't say much. Her mouth was a flat straight line, and I made up my mind that I wouldn't be late again.

Paul leaned over and spoke behind his hand when I slid into my seat. "What happened this time?"

Miss Twitten was watching, so I didn't tell him until breaktime. We had a comprehension test in English, and I got a ninety-eight on it. I thought that might win me a little approval. It didn't, though. Every time Miss Twitten looked at me, or spoke to me, she got that sour look as if she wished they'd put me in someone else's class, not hers.

"Oh, don't worry about it," Paul said carelessly, when I mentioned it to him on the playground. "Old Twit doesn't like anybody. Come on, let's play ball."

So I had to go through that ordeal a third time. Luckily nobody hit anything into right field, so I didn't have to make a fool of myself that way again. I came up to bat, and by some miracle managed to tick the ball. I was so surprised I almost forgot to run until the guys all started yelling at me. I only got to second base before the bell rang, but I felt as if I hadn't been a total disgrace to my team.

Then at noon we all put our lunch sacks down while Paul demonstrated to me how I should be swinging the bat. The other guys all chimed in with advice, and I tried to listen to them all and wondered if I'd ever really get so I was any good at it. I'd be glad when the weather turned bad and we couldn't play baseball any more, I thought.

"Hurry up, let's eat," Steve Baker said. "And then we can play ball." Paul hadn't been kidding when he said that's all the fellows did in this town.

I opened my sack and checked out what Aunt Mattie had put into it. One peanut butter and jelly sandwich, one ham and cheese. An apple and a cupcake with a jolly little face on the top of it, in pink and brown frosting.

I looked at the cupcake and decided I'd wait to eat it until I was on my way home.

"Hey!" Frankie practically snarled, right behind me, so I jumped. "What happened to my lunch? Come on, you guys, that's not funny! Hand it over!"

We all looked at him, innocence written on every face. "Honest," Tubby said. "We didn't take it, Frankie."

"Well, somebody did, 'cause it's not where I left it!"

And then I got that sinking feeling, even before I looked around and saw him. Sure enough, Leroy had known where I was even if he didn't follow me. And he'd picked Frankie's lunch for his own. Even before Frankie spotted him and let out a roar of rage, it was too late. There wasn't anything left but the wrappers and an orange. Leroy only eats oranges if you peel them for him.

Frankie faced me fiercely. I'd thought he looked mean the first time I saw him. He was even worse, now. "OK. It's your dog stole my lunch, give me yours."

I suppose that was only fair. Only I didn't think he had to jerk the bag out of my hand the way he did. He pawed through its contents and came up with the cupcake, the kind Aunt Mattie made for me when I was about three years old.

"Hey, what's this? Look, fellas! Look at the cute cupcake!"

He went on and on about it, laughing, showing it

around, talking baby-talk to me. My face got hot and I would have punched him in the mouth if he hadn't been so much bigger than I was. Besides, my dad says you shouldn't get into fights over trifles. I guessed this was a trifle. I was sure going to tell Aunt Mattie not to decorate any more cupcakes for me, though.

"Oh, go on and eat," Steve said finally. "Or we won't have time to play. Here, Danny, I'll split a tuna fish sandwich with you."

So that's what I had for lunch, along with one of Tubby's candy bars. He always had two or three, so usually he could spare one. His mother must have different ideas about nutrition from Aunt Mattie.

I didn't know what to do about Leroy. He wasn't bothering anybody, now, and even when we played, he just sat on the first-base line, watching. He didn't try to steal the ball again.

I actually managed to catch a pop fly, and then I came up to bat. This time I ticked it, but it didn't go where it was supposed to. It went way up and up and up—and then came down on the other side of the back-up screen and right through the window near-est us.

The window was open, but we heard breaking glass anyway.

Everybody stopped moving to watch it, of course. Paul's voice had a hollow sound. "That's old Twit's room. Golly, Danny!"

I said a bad word, one of my dad's, not one of Gramps's. Leroy leaped up, and before I knew what he was going to do, he was sticking his head through the window, trying to retrieve the ball.

We heard a woman scream, and Frankie said, "Let's get out of here!" We all took off, around the corner of the building, though I didn't know why I was running. Everybody knew I hit the ball, everybody knew Leroy was my dog.

I wondered if my dad would make me stay here when he came back from Ireland.

Mr. Pepper was very understanding. He said he had to run an errand, so he'd take Leroy home for me. And the vase on Miss Twitten's desk belonged to the school, not to her; he said he thought they could absorb the cost of it. However, he pointed out, we were going to have to find some way to keep Leroy away from school.

I said, "Yes, sir," and felt halfway like kicking that dog into the middle of next week and halfway like crying at the thought of him tied up all day. There wasn't any way to make him understand why; that was the hard part, when I knew he didn't really mean any harm.

It started to rain in the middle of the afternoon, and that fitted right in with my mood. There wasn't any baseball game—I didn't know whether I was sorry or glad about that—and I didn't even see C.B. on the way home.

I walked past the old red castle house and of course didn't see anything or anyone there, either. I hoped Miss Rosie hadn't burned her hands too badly, and I wondered if she'd put some kind of fuel in that burning barrel and didn't remember it, or if somebody else had done it. She was lucky she hadn't been seriously hurt, with the fire exploding up out of the barrel that way. I thought of what it would be like to have your hair catch fire, and it was pretty scary.

Leroy was chained on the back porch, waiting for me. He was so tickled he almost knocked me backward down the steps; he quivered all over with happiness.

Gramps opened the screen door. "I guess it didn't work, locking him up until you were gone. He knew where you were, all right. Either followed your scent or just remembered where you went yesterday. We'll have to think of something better."

"Yeah," I said. I let Leroy lick my ear and pretended the ache in my throat didn't mean I was close to tears. "Mr. Pepper says he can't keep coming to school."

"Maybe I can fix a run for him," Gramps said. "Between the shed and the house, over beyond the clothesline. We don't use the clothesline much in the winter, anyway. I've got part of a roll of chicken wire. A run would be better than being on a chain. Come on in, boy, and have a snack to last you until supper. Your Aunt Mattie's been baking sugar cookies."

That was Aunt Mattie's answer to everybody's low spot, I guess. If you broke your leg, she baked you a pie. It wasn't a bad way to cheer somebody up, actually. Not that she knew how I was feeling. About Leroy, and about school in general.

I took half a dozen cookies and sat on the porch looking off through the rain, sharing with Leroy. (He only got a little bit at a time, or he'd have been way ahead of me.)

"Hi, Danny!"

I turned and saw C.B. sloshing toward me through the puddles. She was wearing boots and a yellow slicker with one of those sou'wester hats.

"Hi. Come on up and sit down. You want a cookie?"

"Well, maybe one. I just had a peanut butter sandwich. Boy, I had a lousy day. I heard about you and Leroy. I guess you didn't have such a great day, either."

I moved over to make room for her on the top step; the eaves went out far enough so we didn't get wet.

"My dad talked about how I needed to get to know my peers. So far, it hasn't been anything I couldn't have done without," I said.

"They do everything different here," C.B. said. She flipped the last bite of cookie to Leroy, the same way I did. "For such a little dinky school, they sure take themselves seriously. At least some of the teachers do. I have that Miss Twitten for English and look what she did." She extended her left hand, and I saw a red mark across the back of it. "With her ruler. 'For talking,' she said. Only I wasn't talking, it was the girl behind me, and I never even answered her."

"She doesn't like me, either. Two days of school so far, and I've been late both days. If anything happens tomorrow, she'll probably kill me."

"She'll try to beat you to death with the ruler," C.B. said, and then she spoiled the mood by giggling. "I wish I could have seen her when Leroy came in her window after that ball."

I couldn't enjoy the thought quite as much as she did, knowing it meant Leroy couldn't run loose any more, but I had to smile, anyway.

"Listen, my mother's going to drive into town in a few minutes. Want to go along, and we'll go to the library? About all you can do on a day like this is read."

So I went along, and we each got about a dozen books. For a little town, Indian Lake has a pretty good library. When I came out, a few minutes ahead of C.B., Mr. Holman was passing by on the sidewalk.

He looked at me sort of funny, I thought, though I couldn't imagine why.

"What were you doing over at the Caspitorians' this morning?" he said, coming to a stop. He said it in a sort of nasty way, as if I didn't have any right to have been there.

"Putting out the fire," I said. "Miss Rosie burned her hands, and she was too scared to think of getting the hose and wetting down the shed." He made me feel as if I should step back away from him, but I didn't.

"Well, they don't like people messing around their place," he told me. "So don't you go botherin' 'em." And with that he went striding off in the rain, with his bald spot getting wet.

"Who was that?" C.B. came down the steps behind me, carrying her books in a plastic bag so they wouldn't get wet.

"The guy who lives next to the Cat Ladies. Nice, friendly sort, isn't he?"

"I'll say. Come on, there's Mother," and we made a dash for the car.

I didn't give much thought to Mr. Holman, not right then. Lots of grown-ups were hard to understand, even the ones that mean well. I just figured he was one of them.

4

I made it to school on time the next morning. I left ten minutes earlier than before, and even then I was nervous until I actually reached the school grounds. Paul and Steve were there, and we spent the extra time doing a little batting practice. I didn't feel so self-conscious about it without Frankie there.

"Maybe we could get together and you guys could teach me some more on Saturday," I suggested.

"Well . . ." Paul hesitated. "Well, not this Saturday, Danny. We're having a meeting of the Secret Club. We're going to take our lunches and meet in the park and then go for a hike."

"Oh." I guess my voice sounded sort of flat. "Some other time, then."

"I'm going to put your name up for membership," Paul said. "Tubby and Steve and I will all vote to let you in, and then you can do things with us on weekends."

"What kind of things do you do? Play baseball?"

They both laughed. "No, not at club meetings. We hike and stuff like that. We're going to build a clubhouse in the woods out near the Lodge. A real one that we can put a stove into, and everything. Then we can meet even in the winter. There's lots of wood lying around in the woods we can just pick up, and Tubby's grandmother has an old stove she doesn't use any more. Tubby thinks he can talk her out of it. Then we could even cook out there."

It sounded like fun, having a special clubhouse.

"Who else is in the club?" I wanted to know.

"Well, so far there's only eight of us. Frankie's the president."

I might have known. I wouldn't have bet much on *Frankie* voting me in. The other guys I didn't know anything about.

"It's an honor to get in," Paul said earnestly. "We aren't asking just anybody."

"Why?" I said. "What's wrong with the rest of the seventh grade boys?"

"Well, nothing's *wrong* with them. Only it wouldn't be a special club if everybody was in it, would it?"

I supposed it wouldn't. I guess I have too much imagination, though; I couldn't help thinking how it would feel to the ones who were left out. Still, it was flattering to think that they might want me.

"Uh, Danny," Paul said. "There's one thing. You'll have to go through an initiation, you know. We all did. I mentioned it to Frankie, that maybe what you did that night with the kidnappers ought to count for showing you have courage. But he said that that already happened and we haven't even voted on you yet, so it doesn't count."

I knew what Paul had had to do: he'd had to go, by himself, into a dark and deserted cottage and get something to prove he'd been there. He took a bowling trophy with the man's name on it. Of course, he'd had to return it, too, after he'd showed it to the Secret Club members. But he did *that* in the daylight.

"I guess I can do whatever they decide," I said and hoped it wouldn't be any worse than Paul's initiation.

I sure didn't expect it to be anything like it was, though. I didn't find out until Saturday afternoon what it was going to be.

On Thursday afternoon I got home from school to find a big, fancy car sitting in the driveway.

"Who's that?" C.B. wanted to know.

I shrugged. "Never saw it before. Somebody visiting Aunt Mattie, I suppose. Listen, you want to go for a walk along the lake? I ought to take Leroy for a run after he's been cooped up all day in that pen Gramps built."

C.B. nodded. "O.K. Let's fix a snack, and we can

eat as we go. I'll meet you in fifteen minutes, after I change my clothes."

I went on in the house, and there I met Virgil Caspitorian and his wife, Eleanor. I didn't learn their first names then. Gramps introduced them as Mr. and Mrs. Caspitorian, and I knew *he* must be the nephew of the Cat Ladies who could afford to put a new roof on their house if he cared to.

They looked as if they belonged with that fancy car. He was a big man with a darkish beard; I mean, he had shaved, but his whiskers were so dark he already looked as if he needed another shave. He had very thick black hair, with sideburns artistically touched with silver, as Aunt Mattie said later. He wore a silver-gray suit and a plain red tie.

Aunt Mattie was sort of flustered at having these grand folks in her house; she'd taken them into the front room instead of the kitchen, where we usually sat when the neighbors came over.

Mrs. Caspitorian was younger than her husband, and just as elegant. She had tiny feet and wore shoes that were only a few straps with high heels, and there was a fur collar on her coat even though it wasn't a cold day. Her rings and her earrings were diamonds, I guess; they certainly sparkled, anyway. She was blonde and quite pretty, only somehow when she smiled at me I wasn't at all sure that I liked her.

"We understand you've been to visit Virgil's old aunties," she said.

I looked at Gramps, hoping he might telegraph me some message. He wasn't showing anything in his face. Were they annoyed, as Mr. Holman had been, because I'd been there?

"I didn't exactly visit," I said. "The first time C.B. and I rescued one of their kittens, and the second time there was a fire in the trash barrel that flared up too high, so I got out the hose. That's all."

"Ah, those cats," Mrs. Caspitorian said. "There must be a hundred of them!"

"Thirty-two," I said. "Or maybe thirty-three."

Mrs. Caspitorian forgot to smile. "Really? I should have said far more than that."

I didn't see what difference it made. "They said thirty-two. Or maybe thirty-three."

"Oh, *they* counted them." Her smile came back. "Well, they're getting so old, poor dears. I don't suppose they can remember from one day to the next. So dirty, cats are. The house has such an odor." She looked to Aunt Mattie as if for confirmation of how unpleasant cats were.

Aunt Mattie didn't say anything. I think she was as bewildered as I was.

"I didn't notice any cat odor," I said. "Everything looked clean to me." I didn't mention the dust on a few things. Dust wasn't dirty, and how could two old ladies keep such a big house dusted all the time? "The only smell was the cookies they were baking. It was pretty good."

When she wasn't smiling, Mrs. Caspitorian's mouth was very small. "I can't abide cats," she said in that voice that sounded sweet and yet, somehow, wasn't sweet at all.

Though I didn't dare say so, I couldn't help thinking that since it wasn't her house and she didn't have to take care of the cats, it was none of her business what the old ladies did.

Mr. Caspitorian took over, then. "You say you stepped in and put out a fire yesterday morning, young man."

"Well, not exactly," I said. "The fire was in the trash barrel, and it was dying down so it didn't seem dangerous. I didn't squirt any water on it. Just on the grass and the shed, so they couldn't catch fire, too."

"But I understand Aunt Rosie started the fire with gasoline, or some such thing?"

Now how could he know that? "She said she didn't," I told him. I wasn't sure what he was getting at, but I didn't think I was going to like it.

It took a while, with some more questions and answers, before we found out what they were leading up to.

They thought it was time Miss Rosie and Miss Anna were put into a home for old people, and their house closed up.

"Dangerous old place," Mrs. Caspitorian said. "A fire hazard."

"I'm sorry to see it happen," her husband added,

"but they're getting senile."

I knew *senile* meant they were getting so old they didn't think very well any more.

"They didn't seem senile to me," I said and kept on talking even though Mrs. Caspitorian's mouth got all tight and small again. "They were keeping house and making cookies and taking care of their cats."

She gave me a look that was pure venom. That's poison, like a snake has when he bites you. She turned to Gramps.

"I'm sure you can understand, Mr. Minden, that we're only concerned with their welfare. We want what's best for them."

"Oh, sure," Gramps said. "Usually, seems to me, the best thing for old folks is to leave them alone in their own homes, long as they aren't a danger to themselves or anyone else."

"That's just it, sir," Virgil Caspitorian said, and he was beginning to sound sort of grim, too. "We think they *are* a danger to themselves. And, possibly, to someone else."

Aunt Mattie was looking rather pink, the way she does when she wants to say something and thinks maybe it would be better if she didn't.

"I don't suppose a *boy* would recognize senility," Mrs. Caspitorian said. "They *are*, you know. They talk to themselves all the time. And to those horrid cats, as if they were human."

Gramps chuckled. "If they shut up everybody that ever talked to themselves, wouldn't be very many people still running loose. And I expect dogs and cats need to be talked to same as human beings. Ain't that right, Leroy?"

Leroy thumped his tail on the floor and let his tongue hang way out.

Mrs. Caspitorian's face turned red.

"We came here," Mr. Caspitorian said, "in the hope that since your grandson has had some contact with the old ladies recently, you would be willing to testify to the oddity of their habits."

Aunt Mattie's jaw sagged. "You mean, you want to go to court and get some judge to say they should be put in a home?"

"For their own good," Mrs. Caspitorian said.

"Well," Gramps told them, "I haven't seen enough of your aunts lately to know, one way or the other. But Danny, here, doesn't think they need to be locked up, so I reckon they're all right the way they are, for a while yet."

"We don't mean to lock them up!" Mrs. Caspitorian protested. "We want to settle them in a nice, modern rest home, with other people their own age, where there are nurses to take care of them and see to their meals and—"

"Same thing, ain't it?" Gramps said cheerfully. "Same as being in a jail, to somebody used to doing what he wants. I don't think we can help you folks."

They talked a few minutes more. It didn't do them any good. When they drove away in their big, shining car, Gramps looked after them and said thoughtfully, "Senile! Rosie's the same age I am, and Anna's only two years older! I'll bet you the only reason they want them out of that house is so they can go in and search for that money old man Caspitorian hid, years ago."

I looked at him curiously. "Why would they need to do that, Gramps? They have plenty of money of their own."

Gramps laughed. "Couple things you'll learn, boy. One is that the people who have lots of money want lots more of it. And the other is that people driving big cars and wearing diamond rings don't necessarily have all that stuff paid for."

He was chuckling to himself when he went back inside.

I told C.B. about the Caspitorians when we went for our walk along the lake. She was as indignant as I was about what the Cat Ladies' nephew wanted to do.

"He won't be able to do it, will he?"

"Not if he depends on people like Gramps to testify about them," I said, and then we forgot about it and just enjoyed ourselves.

Saturday morning Gramps and I went to town to run some errands for Aunt Mattie, and while we were in the hardware store, something caught fire in the back room.

It was just some packing stuff someone had left there instead of carrying it out to the trash bin in the alley, but it got pretty hot before the firemen came and put it out. The owner of the store wiped his forehead and then gave Gramps a funny look.

"You know, Charlie, it's not that I don't appreciate having you for a customer, but it seems like it's dangerous."

"Oh?" Gramps stared right back at him. "How's that, Amos?"

"Everywhere you go, funny things happen. Like that fire. Luckily it only damaged a few cartons of stuff, not my entire store. I just got to wondering if it started because of you and that confounded curse of yours."

Gramps put up a restraining hand. "Hey, you got it all wrong! I don't *cause* things to happen! I just wander on the spot where things are going on. You have to admit it must have been smoldering back there before I got here, or it wouldn't have burst into flames about two minutes after I walked through the door. Instead of blaming me, why don't you blame that young feller that didn't have sense enough to haul all that packing material outside instead of leaving it near your water heater."

The hardware store owner sighed. "Oh, I guess

you're right. Makes a person wonder, though."

On the way home, I asked Gramps if he was going to tell Aunt Mattie about the fire. I knew she'd get that pinched look around her mouth if he did.

Gramps grunted. "Well, if I tell her, she'll be annoyed. She hates that Minden Curse business, as if I had any control over it, you know. But if I don't tell her, someone else will, sooner or later. And when she finds out I was there and didn't tell her before it comes out in the paper, why that'll bother her even more. So I guess I'll tell her myself and get it over with."

I didn't care to be around when he did it, so I went out and sat on the back steps. I was there when Paul came to tell me what the Secret Club had decided. In fact, they all came, the ones I knew: Frankie and Steve and Tubby. They had taken their hike out past our place and stopped on the way back.

Leroy went romping out to meet them, wagging his tail. Nobody minded that he was smelling around their pockets for leftovers, except Frankie. "Why don't you lock that mutt up?" Frankie said.

Leroy had been locked up most of the week, and I wasn't going to put him back in the pen just on Frankie's say-so. "Come, Leroy," I said. "Sit!"

Leroy obediently lowered his rump to the ground and kept on wagging his tail. Tubby, who is never without a few bites to eat, searched his pockets and came up with a rather squashed half a sandwich and let Leroy lick his fingers for the crumbs.

"We voted to admit you to the Secret Club," Paul said. "If you pass the initiation, of course."

"Well, good. What is it I have to do?" I looked around the circle of faces. They were all smiling, even Frankie, only his smile looked different from the others, and in a minute, I found out why.

"Frankie's president, so he gets to say what the initiation is," Paul said.

"Danny's a special case," Frankie said, grinning more widely. "He's already a hero, right? He's had his picture in the paper with his super dog and all that stuff. So he should have a special initiation, right?"

I began to get the idea that maybe I wasn't going to like this too much. I wasn't really a hero. All that stuff just sort of accidentally happened to me. I also had the notion that Frankie didn't like me very much; he liked being the center of attention himself.

"I think Danny's good enough," Frankie said, still grinning in that horrid way, "so he should be able to—" He paused for dramatic effect, as if he were on the stage and flaring a cape over his shoulder to impress the audience. "—to bring us one of the Cat Ladies' pets."

For a few seconds nobody said anything. That didn't sound so terrible, since there were plenty of them, and they were all over the place. Everybody was still looking pleasant and pleased that I was going to join them.

And then Frankie added the capper. "A special one of them. Danny's going to bring us . . . *Killer*."

The smiles stayed put for about ten seconds, and then they started sliding off faces like butter melting into a hot pancake. I don't know what I looked like, but I was having a sudden mental image of that cat: big, black, tough.

Paul made a little squeaking sound. "Aw, hey, Frankie . . . *Killer?*"

"Killer," Frankie said. "Maybe your dog will help you, Danny."

Tubby forgot to chew on whatever it was he was eating. "Nobody's ever been able to get near Killer," he said, as if Frankie didn't already know that. "Remember the time he was hit by the car and they had to take him to the vet? Even Steve's dad couldn't handle him until they put him to sleep. They had a terrible time with him!"

That was the first I knew that Steve's dad was the veterinarian. Not that knowing it helped me much.

Frankie was enjoying himself, and I suspected right then that he didn't really want me in the Secret Club at all. I mean, why give me something to do that was practically impossible, if he hoped I'd be able to do it?

Still, if I backed out now, said I didn't want to be in their old club anyway, they'd all think I was a coward. I didn't doubt that by Monday morning every kid in school would know I'd chickened out. I wondered if my dad had any idea what a bunch he was throwing me to when he decided I ought to go to school here for a year.

Steve shifted from one foot to the other. "That's a pretty tough assignment, Frankie. Tougher than the rest of us had."

"Well, Danny Minden is some sort of super hero, isn't he? You wouldn't expect a super hero to do just an ordinary thing like steal a church bell and hang it in the park, would you?"

I was beginning to figure it out. Frankie didn't want to be the bad guy by voting to keep me out of the club. No, he wanted *me* to be the one to keep myself out, because I couldn't do the initiation stunt he'd set for me.

"OK," I said and hoped I didn't sound the way I felt. "How long do I have to do this? To capture Killer and bring him to the club members?"

"Oh, say a week," Frankie said, but the others all made troubled sounds over that. It was Steve who put it into words.

"It's a tough assignment, Frankie. I think he ought to have more time than that."

For a minute I thought Frankie would argue with that. After all, he was used to being the boss, and he wanted to make it as hard for me as he could. Then I guess he looked at all their faces and saw that the others agreed with Steve.

Frankie shrugged. "OK, then. Make it two weeks. Only he doesn't come to the Secret Club or help with the clubhouse until he passes the test." He sort of smirked at me; no doubt he figured that would keep me out forever.

"Fair enough," I said, before anybody else could comment on it. "And where do I take Killer when I get him?"

"To anybody in the club," Steve said quickly, before Frankie could set up another roadblock. "Any one of the four of us, anyway."

"Any time, day or night?"

"Any time, day or night," Steve confirmed. "Right, guys?"

So that was the way they left it.

I didn't realize I was shaking until they'd all disappeared down the road.

5

C.B. just looked at me with her mouth hanging open when I told her. "Why, that's not a fair thing to ask anybody to do! I think that Frankie is a stinker!"

I thought so, myself, but that didn't make any difference.

"Why don't you tell them to go jump in the lake?" C.B. suggested. "What's so great about their stupid old club, anyway?"

"I don't know if it is special. Only these guys are the only ones I've made friends with so far—"

"Some friends," C.B. interrupted.

"Yeah, well, I think Paul and Steve and Tubby like me. And if I don't do the initiation thing, they'll all say I'm afraid of a cat."

"So are they," C.B. said. "I'll bet none of them would try to catch Killer."

I didn't figure they would, either. It didn't make any difference. Either I tried, or I forgot about being part of their gang. I already knew that most of the kids in my class spent all their time playing ball, or the guys had their Secret Club activities. If I didn't get in, I'd find myself on the sidelines, maybe for the whole year.

C.B. was looking at me strangely. "Are you going to do it, then? Try to catch Killer?"

"I guess so," I said. "What else can I do?"

Deciding to try and deciding *how* to try were two different things.

After church on Sunday (I'd learned that at our house you had to be practically dead before you were allowed to stay home from church), I told Aunt Mattie I'd walk home, I needed the exercise.

"Well, dinner will be ready around two," Aunt Mattie said. "Try to be home for that. It's roast and mashed potatoes, and I still have some fresh corn on the cob."

I didn't really need the exercise, of course. I could tell Gramps didn't think so, either, but he didn't ask me what I really was going to do. Gramps is pretty neat that way.

The truth was that I'd decided, right in the middle of church, that the first thing to do was reconnoiter. I had always liked that word. It meant I was going to sort of casually stroll by the red wooden castle and look things over, see what the situation was. See if there was any way I could figure to get close to that cat.

Actually, it wasn't so difficult to get close enough to *see* him. Killer was sitting on top of the gate post, right where I had first spotted him.

He must weigh twenty pounds, I thought. I stopped a few yards away and looked at him.

Killer looked right back, his amber eyes closed into mean little slits. He looked as if he'd just as soon sink his claws into me as not.

I had known a lady who'd had her cat's claws removed so they couldn't claw up her good furniture. It was never allowed outside, so it didn't need claws to climb trees and catch mice and things like that.

Nobody had removed Killer's claws. They looked a mile long. I almost flinched just thinking how it would feel if he sank them into my arm or my face. Yet how the heck could I pick him up without getting those claws into me?

And besides his claws, he had teeth. Almost as if he knew what I was thinking, he spat at me, and I could see them. They were enough to give a guy cold chills.

I could just see Frankie at home, laughing his head off at how clever he'd been keeping me out of the Secret Club by giving me an impossible task to do.

But was it impossible?

Maybe I could make friends with Killer.

I cleared my throat. "Hi, Killer." And then I remembered, his name was really Chester. "Hi, Chester," I said.

It sounded silly. No creature that was as mean-looking as that cat could be called Chester.

The cat didn't move. He didn't even blink those slitted eyes. He stared at me the way he would at a mouse he intended to eat in about two minutes.

"I'll make a deal with you," I said. "You come along with me to visit those Secret Club guys, and I'll buy you some liver with my next allowance. A whole pound of it."

Killer didn't move. He didn't even twitch his tail.

"Maybe it would be worthwhile," I said conversationally, "if I brought you some liver ahead of time. On account, sort of. Do you like liver?"

If I'd had to guess what he was thinking, I'd have voted for "Danny Minden, on a platter." One thing sure, old Killer wasn't going to be easy.

Still, maybe it wasn't impossible. Maybe he could be won over.

The voice behind me nearly startled me out of my socks. It must have startled Killer, too, because he shot off the branch and raced across the lawn toward the house.

"What're you doing hanging around here? I hope you aren't making a nuisance of yourself, bothering those old ladies."

I settled down after a few seconds and found my voice. "I'm allowed to walk past on the sidewalk, aren't I? I mean, it's a public sidewalk."

Mr. Holman looked almost as mean as Killer.

"You don't get sassy with me, young man. You go on, get on your way."

I guess I would have gone—after all, he was bigger than I was, and besides I knew Aunt Mattie would have a fit if I was deliberately rude to an adult, no matter how much he deserved it—except that just then the front door of the red house opened and Miss Rosie came out on the steps.

"Oh, hello, there!" she called out. "Hello, Mr. Holman. Hello, young man." She came down the path toward us. When she got close enough, I could see the singed ends of the hairs around her face. She hadn't bandaged her hands—sometimes, if they aren't burned too badly and you get them into ice water fast enough, you don't have blisters—but they were reddened, and I was sure they were tender.

"I saw Danny out here," she said. "Did I remember your name right? Danny? And I thought you might be of some help to me, if you wouldn't mind?"

"Anything you need," Mr. Holman said quickly, "you just let me know, Miss Rosie. I'm right handy, next door. Mow your grass or anything."

"Oh, what I need isn't a job for a man," Miss Rosie said. "Ordinarily, I'd do it myself. I did hurt my hands, though, so I'm being careful what I do for a few days. I need some jars brought up from the basement, and I don't want to lift the boxes myself just yet. We're making jelly, you know. I can't pay you anything, I'm afraid," she said to me, "but maybe you'd like some of the jelly when it's done. We're doing apple, now, and by next week we can begin on the grapes."

"I can do that for you—" Mr. Holman began, but I wasn't going to pass up an opportunity to get closer to Killer. Frankie probably expected me to just wade in and try to grab him and get all scratched up for my efforts. I knew better than that. Capturing Killer was going to take strategy, and that meant some planning. What better way to start than getting inside the house and making friends with him?

"I'd be glad to carry up your jars," I said and was glad Aunt Mattie couldn't hear me interrupting Mr. Holman. "And I especially like grape jelly."

"I knew you were the kind of boy who likes to help people," Miss Rosie said and smiled at her silent neighbor (who didn't smile back) before she led the way into the house.

She made me feel a little ashamed, because I was intending to help myself, too. On the other hand, I *was* helping her.

The cats milled around on the porch when we went up the steps, all of them looking clean and brushed and elegant in their fancy collars. A regal gray tabby with a lavender collar rubbed against my legs when we went inside, following along. I didn't see Killer anywhere.

"I think Polly likes you," Miss Rosie said, sounding pleased. "It's back this way. We get into the cellar from the kitchen. It's such a little job, I didn't ask Mr. Holman. He's been very helpful these past few weeks, and his wife, too. Even offered to come and clean house for us! I told her, my goodness, we're still able to keep up with the house cleaning!" She ran a finger along the top of a table in the hallway, inspected the dust it left, and wiped it on her skirt, leaving a little smear. "Good enough, anyway. Nobody sees it but us and the cats. Besides, we couldn't afford to pay anyone to clean for us. I don't think a smidgeon of dust hurts anything, do you?"

She didn't wait for an answer, but led the way through the big kitchen to the cellar door. Miss Anna was there in her wheelchair, drinking a cup of tea at the big table.

"Say hello to Danny, Anna," Miss Rosie said raising her voice. "He's going to bring up the jelly glasses for us."

"Hello," Miss Anna said. She didn't sound friendly, especially. It wasn't until we had gone all the way down the narrow, steep stairs into a musty-smelling basement that Miss Rosie apologized for her sister.

"You mustn't mind Anna if she sounds short. She doesn't mean anything by it. It's only that she's in pain a good deal of the time. She has severe arthritis, and it makes her hands ache. Since her legs don't work any more, she has to do everything with her hands, and it depresses her when they ache. It doesn't bother her as much when it's sunny. Actually, I think she'd be all right most of the time if we could get the furnace fixed."

She chattered away as I followed her through a maze of packing crates, old furniture, and spider webs. She didn't even seem to notice when she walked through one of the webs and a spider landed in her hair and crawled down onto her collar, until I reached over and brushed it off.

Then she only smiled. "All kinds of creatures down here, aren't there? There, over against that wall, there are the jelly glasses. See? Two boxes of them."

"What's wrong with the furnace?" I asked. It was cold and damp down there, and I could imagine the entire house being that way when it got to be winter.

"I don't know. It just stopped working last spring. We've made do with the woodstove in the kitchen and the little Franklin stove in the parlor in the evenings. I don't suppose you even know what a parlor is, do you? They call them living rooms, these days. Can you lift that all right?"

The boxes weren't heavy, but they were bulky

enough that I had to take one box at a time. When I got them both upstairs, I washed my hands in the kitchen sink and accepted their thanks. The gray tabby named Polly jumped up beside me and rubbed against my arm.

"My, she does take to you! I guess she's lonely today. That Chester is usually her favorite of the cats, but he's been gone since last night. I do hope he isn't into mischief again."

Chester—or Killer—was a buddy of Polly's? I looked at the tabby with new appreciation. She was perfectly happy to have me stroke her sleek fur; she vibrated under my hand, purring as if she had a motor running inside of her. "She's a nice cat," I said, quite sincerely. "And K—I mean, Chester's OK. I just saw him out front."

"They're all nice," Miss Rosie assured me. "And all different, such personalities. Well, thank you, Danny. You've been a big help. We'll let you know when the jelly is ready."

I was disappointed, when I let myself out the front door, that Killer hadn't come inside. But maybe there was some way I could use knowing Polly to my advantage. I'd have to think about it.

I wasn't actually any nearer to knowing how to capture Killer, though. If there was a strategy that would work, I hadn't thought of it yet. Killer had been hostile to me from the minute we met, spitting and showing his teeth. Making friends with him was probably impossible, but catching him *without* making friends first sounded even less likely. So, if Polly was Killer's good friend, maybe she was a step in the right direction, even if I couldn't yet see how. Besides, who could fail to like a cat that acted as if she thought you were wonderful?

When I walked through the cats on the porch, I glanced over and saw the Holmans watching me. I decided I'd rather be around the cats.

I pretended I didn't notice them and let myself out through the front gate. And then I saw him. Killer. Watching me from that low branch that overhung the sidewalk.

Something peculiar fluttered in my stomach. I swallowed, and then I thought, what the heck, he's only a cat.

"Hi, Killer. I mean, Chester." My voice sounded normal, I thought. He couldn't hate all human beings; he responded to Miss Rosie and Miss Anna. Could I win him over if I really worked at it?

He stared at me with those amber eyes, the sun glittering off the stones in his collar, his fur thick and sleek.

"How'd you like to be friends?" I asked.

He didn't say anything, so I got braver and moved up close enough to touch him, only I wasn't ready to do that, yet.

"Your friend Polly likes me," I told him. "And when I don't have Leroy with me, there's nothing menacing about me. I won't hurt you."

He had been licking one paw, but he paused then and looked at me, and I swear he understood what I was saying. His expression was as readable as Leroy's was sometimes, and I knew what it said.

Don't try to kid me, buster.

"No, really," I said. "All you'd have to do would be to come with me to one of the members of the Secret Club, be a gentleman for half an hour or so. And then I wouldn't bother you again."

Killer went back to licking his foot, which was already spotless. I couldn't think of him as Chester; it an absurd name for him. I had to call him Killer, the way the other kids did.

"I'll come and see you again," I told him. "Next time I'll bring you a treat. What do you like? Liver? Tuna fish? I could catch you a mouse, but you'd probably rather catch your own. Remember, though, I'll be back. I didn't scare you off this time, did I? You and I are going to get acquainted."

I didn't know if my talk had done any good, but so far he hadn't seemed too terrible. Maybe it was only dogs he hated.

I stood there for a minute and then impulsively put out a hand toward him.

I guess I should have done it more slowly. Or

maybe not at all. Because Killer, who had been calmly washing his leg, suddenly slashed out with his claws.

I jerked my hand back and looked at the blood oozing up in the scratch marks.

Well, I thought, I had known it wasn't going to be easy. Now I was sure of it.

I hated to go to school the next day and have every-body see those marks on my hand. The others didn't say anything, but Frankie did. I might have guessed it would be Frankie.

"Hey!" he said at morning break time. "Look at old Danny! Looks like he's not having much luck catching Killer, doesn't it?"

I didn't say anything, and the other guys just looked at me. Steve was the one who said what they were all probably thinking. "It was a tough initiation stunt, Frankie. Killer's too dangerous for Danny to try to catch. Maybe we ought to—"

Frankie's smile disappeared in a hurry. "We don't change it. We set it, and that's it. Either he brings us Killer or he doesn't get into the Secret Club."

I could tell that the others didn't like it. They

weren't going to argue with him about it, though.

"You give up?" Frankie asked, grinning again now that everybody had knuckled under.

"No," I told him. "I still have the rest of my two weeks, don't I?"

"Sure. Sure, why not? Six o'clock, Saturday after next. Lots of luck, Danny," Frankie said. He was still chuckling as he moved out onto the ball field.

I had two weeks, and I guessed I'd need every bit of it. Maybe I wouldn't succeed even then, but at least I'd have tried. They couldn't say I was a quitter or a coward. Although, I reflected wryly, maybe it would be better to be thought a coward than to have Killer rake those claws across my face; he could blind me. I was glad I'd only stuck out my hand where he could reach it.

C.B. wanted to know what I was going to try next. "Maybe you could get him in a cage," she suggested. "They didn't say you couldn't do that, did they? We could make a cage. Or we could use Marcella's cat box, the one we use to carry her to the vet when she needs a shot or something."

"How do we get him into it?" I asked. "Send him an engraved invitation?"

"Lure him in with something he likes to eat," C.B. said. "Marcella will go in, for a bit of liver. At least, she did the first time. Now we have to pretend to feed her and not show her the box until we get our hands on her."

"Marcella's tame. Killer's wild," I pointed out.

"Not totally wild. He lets the Caspitorian sisters handle him, doesn't he? They must have put that collar on him. And I'm sure they brush him; he couldn't look so sleek and smooth if they didn't. Shall we try it?"

I was glad C.B. was on my side. I didn't quite know how to say so, though, so I just grunted. "OK. Let's try it. You get the cat box."

We decided to do it after school on Tuesday. I was sort of dubious when I saw the box. I didn't know if we could keep Killer in it once we got him there— if we ever did—because it was only made of cardboard, and I remembered Killer's long claws.

We weren't sure what to do with the box during school hours. Without discussing it, we agreed that it would be better if nobody knew what we were up to, so we couldn't carry the cat box around in the open.

So C.B. wrapped it up right then in a green plastic garbage bag, which we took turns carrying because the box was bulky and we couldn't use the handle when it was inside the bag. And we hid the whole thing in the bushes at the corner near the Caspitorians' house.

On the way home we talked about bait. I had decided that liver was probably the most enticing bait I could use. I had planned to go over to the market and buy some right after school, until I found out how much liver costs per pound. Dad had given Gramps money so I could have an allowance, but I'd already spent last week's plus my savings for a baseball glove (maybe if I had one I could catch better, and it seemed I had to play ball if I was going to live in Indian Lake) and I couldn't wait until next Saturday for the next allowance.

"Wouldn't your grampa give you an advance on the allowance?" C.B. had asked, when we talked about it on Monday.

"Sure. But he'd probably ask me why I needed it. Gramps is pretty understanding, for a grown-up, but I've got a hunch he wouldn't think much of trying to catch Killer in a cat box."

She thought about that and then nodded reluctantly. "Yeah. You're right. But what'll we do, then? We'll never get him into the box unless there's something in there he can't resist. Do you suppose he likes egg salad sandwiches? That's what I've got today, and there was some left over so that's what I'll get tomorrow, too."

"And I'll have peanut butter and jelly. Aunt Mattie rotates so I'll have variety, but I always have peanut butter and jelly—or maybe honey—on Tuesdays."

We stared at each other. "We'd have a lot better

chance with liver. Listen, I know what. I'm sure Aunt Mattie has some in the freezer. I'll bet she wouldn't miss it if I took just a sliver or so of it. When she opens a package, she always cooks more than we can eat."

So that was what I did. I waited until Aunt Mattie was busy on the phone, talking to her friend Aggie Kirk on the extension in the living room, and I opened up the freezer and found a package of liver. At first I couldn't cut it because it was frozen too hard, but C.B. had said it didn't have to be completely defrosted.

"Just a little, and then you can slice it. My mom does," she said.

So I took the package out onto the back porch and put it at the side of the steps where it would be hidden by a little bush in case Aunt Mattie came outside again that evening, though that wasn't likely. Once she got started talking to Aggie, Gramps said, she didn't know when to quit. They were usually good for an hour, anyway.

I went over to C.B.'s, then, and we watched a western movie on TV. We'd both seen it before, but we watched it again. When her mother called in to say that was enough television for one evening, C.B. turned off the set. "Let's check and see if you can cut the liver yet," she suggested.

It was getting dark when we walked over to our

house along the beach. There were lights on in the kitchen; when we peeked in the window, only Gramps was there, rocking and carving something. He carved a bird in a cage once, and now it looked as if he was making a ship.

"We should have thought to bring a knife," C.B. said, backing away before Gramps could look up and see us.

"I've got my jackknife." I dug it out of my pocket. "And one of those plastic bags to put it in, the ones you press together at the top like a zipper so it seals the bag. It's a good thing we didn't wait any longer, or it would have been too dark to see." I bent over and poked around under the bush. "Where's the package? I thought I put it right here . . ."

C.B. leaned past me. "Well, it's not there now."

I straightened up with a sudden horrid suspicion. "Where's Leroy?"

C.B. made a moaning sound. "Oh, no! He couldn't have! Could he?"

"I didn't think he'd smell it when it was frozen solid that way. Leroy! Leroy, where are you?"

He didn't come. We found him, two minutes later, looking guilty but happy, with shreds of white wrapping paper clinging to his whiskers, lying against the side of the house.

"Oh, you rotten dog! How could you eat it when it was hard as a rock?" I demanded. Part of the paper was there, with a few reddish smears on it. The rest was gone, including the wrappings. I wondered if he could digest plastic wrap and wrapping paper or if it would make him sick.

"He chews up bones," C.B. said. "I guess he could handle frozen liver. Didn't he leave any of it?"

"Nothing. Not a taste," I said through my teeth. I glared at him, and Leroy had the grace to hang his head. It wasn't very convincing though, because he wagged his tail.

"What do we do now?" C.B. wondered. "I'd get some, but we don't have any in our freezer. The best I could do would be a can of tuna, and I'm not sure I could get it without Mom knowing about it. I don't think she'd approve of trying to catch Killer, either."

I resisted the urge to strangle Leroy. "I guess it's really my own fault for leaving it in a place where he could get at it. Well, I'll have to see if there's any more in the freezer. How many packages of liver would there be in a side of beef, anyway? I know we've already had it twice since I've been here."

"You can't get it now without your grandfather seeing you," C.B. observed. "Maybe he'd understand, Danny."

"No. I don't dare take a chance. Because if he says *no*, then where will I be? I'll just have to wait until they've both gone to bed."

So C.B. went on home, and I went in the house. Leroy followed me in and sniffed around his dish as if he hadn't just eaten a pound or two of liver.

"Hungry, eh?" Gramps asked him, and put some dry dog food in the pie pan. "Nobody around here takes care of you but me, do they, boy? That Danny, all he thinks about is his own stomach." He looked at me slyly, grinning, because he knew I always gave Leroy some of what I was eating, at least when Aunt Mattie wasn't watching.

I couldn't quite manage to grin back. Sometimes it is hard to maintain a sense of humor around Leroy.

I didn't get a chance to find another package of liver for over an hour. Then finally Aunt Mattie and Gramps both went upstairs. They thought I was already asleep; I'd gone to my room and turned off the lights. I had stretched out on the bed and begun to think about what I was trying to do, wondering if it was worth it, getting into the Secret Club.

When the line of light under my door went out, I waited five minutes and then crept back into the kitchen. I used a flashlight, because I didn't want Aunt Mattie to notice that the lights were back on, and I found a second package of liver. I hoped Aunt Mattie didn't know how many there had been in there.

This time, I put the package in a pan with a lid on it and took it into my bedroom and put it where

Leroy couldn't get at it. By the time my alarm went off in the morning, I could hack off several strips of the liver and seal it in the plastic bag. I put the rest of it back into a corner of the freezer and hoped that by the time Aunt Mattie discovered that the package had been opened, I'd have a good explanation ready for her. I supposed the truth would be all right, once I'd succeeded in what I was trying to do.

The liver, in the plastic bag, was in my pocket the next day when I went to school. I'd considered putting it into my lunch sack, but a couple of times Frankie had grabbed my lunch and dumped it out where everybody could see it. I don't know what made him think he had a right to do that with someone else's lunch, but with Frankie you didn't make an issue of things unless you were prepared to get just as nasty as *he* could get. So far, I had tried to avoid open warfare, although it was a temptation to do something to get even with him.

It began to rain just before break time. Paul and Tubby and Steve and Frankie were depressed because we weren't going to be able to go outside and play ball. I was sort of relieved, because even with the new glove I wasn't any good as a ball player.

"We will have a quiet time here in the classroom," Miss Twitten said. "You may read or draw or talk quietly among yourselves."

"Read!" Frankie said in horror. "Holy cow!"

Across the aisle from me, Paul muttered under his breath, "Frankie doesn't read very well."

Steve, who sat in front of me, turned around. "Have you tried to catch Killer yet, Danny?"

I shrugged, not wanting to admit to anything.

"I hope you get him. It *was* him that scratched your hand, wasn't it?"

"I wasn't trying to catch him," I said. "Just be friendly."

"I've seen Miss Rosie pick him up, and once I saw him in Miss Anna's lap when she had her chair on the front porch. I don't think he ever lets anyone else touch him, though." Steve frowned faintly. "It isn't really a fair initiation. But you know Frankie—he never backs down."

"What you going to do, Danny? Read?" Paul asked.

"Yeah, I guess so. If there's anything good left on the shelf." We had a library down the hall, but we also had a shelf of books along one window ledge; a lot of the kids had already gone over to pick out something, and I figured by the time I got there I'd be lucky to find a copy of *The Bobbsey Twins* left.

I decided to try, though. I went over and picked out a book about sports, thinking maybe I'd get some hints on how to play ball. When I started back, I went right past Frankie's desk, and that was a mistake.

If I'd thought about it, I'd have taken the long

way around. Only I didn't, and when Frankie stuck his foot out in front of me at the last second, I tripped and fell sprawling across the floor.

I hit hard, knocking all the wind out of me. It was so unexpected I hardly even got a chance to cushion my fall with my hands.

Behind me, Frankie sniggered. I wasn't hurt, but I was mad, the kind of mad that made me want to get up and hit him. I guess that's why I stayed there for a few seconds, fighting back the urge to show Frankie what it was like to be on the receiving end of things for once.

Miss Twitten's voice was sharp. "Danny Minden, you get up immediately. I will not tolerate this rough-housing in my classroom! Go to your seat and stay there!"

This was so unfair I jerked my head up to look at her in astonishment as I scrambled to my feet. Did she think I'd done it on purpose?"

"I will not have people in here who cannot behave," the teacher said. "If you continue to disrupt the class, I will ask Mr. Pepper to make other arrangements for you troublemakers."

And then, when I'd regained my feet, Miss Twitten suddenly got a look of horror across her face. In fact, she actually turned pale.

"Oh, good heavens! How badly are you hurt? What did you fall on?"

I wasn't hurt at all, and I started to say so, but she didn't let me. "You, Steve Baker, go see if the school nurse is in! And you'd better call Mr. Pepper, too! Here, Danny, sit down! Let me unbutton your shirt and see how serious it is!"

And only then did I realize that my shirt front was wet. I looked down and saw it, the spreading wet red stain.

7

I felt the heat rise in my face as I realized what had happened.

"No, wait, I'm not hurt, it's only . . . it's only . . ."

The panic faded out of Miss Twitten's expression, and the look that followed was worse. Fury, anger strong enough so she wanted to do to me what I'd wanted to do to Frankie.

"That isn't blood on your shirt?" she demanded.

"Well, yes. Only it's not *my* blood, it's . . ." How could I explain? Particularly right there in front of the whole class?

"Go to the office," she said tightly. "And perhaps it would be just as well if you didn't come back into the class at all."

What did that mean? Was I being expelled because

that rotten old Frankie had tripped me and made the plastic bag of liver I was carrying come open? It must have broken the seal when I fell on it, and the juice in it squirted up and through my shirt, but there was no way I could be responsible for that. It would have been perfectly all right, and no one would have known I had the little pieces of liver in my pocket, if Frankie hadn't tripped me. And she wasn't saying anything to him at all!

"Tell Mr. Pepper," Miss Twitten said, "that you have been a disruptive influence in my classroom and that I refuse to permit any more of it."

Steve, still standing by the doorway, gave me a look of sympathy. I didn't know if he'd seen what happened or not, but he certainly knew I hadn't deliberately done anything to disrupt the class.

"You may sit down, Steven," Miss Twitten said and turned her back on me.

I stood there for a minute, but there didn't seem to be anything to do except leave. The other kids had laughed, at first, the same as Frankie; now they were all quiet, staring. Maybe some of them had thought I was hurt, too.

I clamped my teeth together and walked out of the room and down the hall toward the principal's office. Maybe I'd ought to go wash out my shirt first, I thought. On the other hand, Mr. Pepper might understand better if he saw what I looked like right now. If there was any chance of anybody understanding anything.

Mr. Pepper stood up behind his desk when I walked in. I guess he saw immediately that I wasn't in serious condition, though, because after a few seconds he sat back down.

He sighed. "Are you in trouble again, Danny?"

"Yes. I didn't do anything, though. Miss Twitten says I disrupted the class; but somebody tripped me and I fell, and the plastic bag I was carrying the liver in broke open."

He tapped his teeth with a pencil. "You were carrying a bag of liver. Raw liver, obviously. Would you care to explain to me why, Danny?"

I considered that for a few seconds. What could I say that wouldn't sound completely crazy? Not to mention getting the guys in the Secret Club into trouble too, possibly. Frankie would deserve it, of course. Only I had a hunch that tattling on other kids wasn't the way to get accepted at Indian Lake School, no matter what Frankie had done.

"No, sir," I said finally. "I don't think I care to explain."

He had put down the pencil and now made a tent with his fingers. He looked at me thoughtfully. "I see. You do have a good reason, other than to annoy Miss Twitten, for carrying a plastic bag of raw liver."

"Well, it was still pretty nearly frozen when I put

it in the bag," I said. "And it didn't have much juice—I mean blood—on it then. And if I hadn't fallen on it, the bag wouldn't have come open, and nobody would have known I had it."

He nodded. "I see. And I don't suppose you'd care to tell me who tripped you, either?"

I could have lied and said I didn't know. Or I could have given Frankie's name and let *him* come to the office. Instead of either, I said, "No, sir."

He sighed again. "Well. I believe you didn't plan this episode. Do you think you can wash out that shirt so that it will be acceptable in Miss Twitten's room for the rest of the day?"

I swallowed. "Yes, sir. Only I don't think she wants me to come back to her class." How could I explain it at home if they kicked me out of school altogether?

"I'll speak to Miss Twitten myself. You wash out your clothes—and maybe it would be a good idea if you put the liver in the refrigerator in the teacher's lounge. Do you know where it is? And then rejoin your classmates when the bell rings."

He got up, and I knew I'd been dismissed. I went along to the lavatory and cleaned my shirt the best I could; the stain didn't all come out, but at least I didn't look as if I was the victim of an axe murderer. I considered throwing the liver out, only I couldn't, really, because it was the best thing I'd been able to think of to catch Killer. So I resealed the plastic bag and put it in the refrigerator until after school.

The way things were going, my year at Indian Lake was going to be a long one.

C.B. was waiting on the corner after I'd collected the liver. I didn't have to explain the kind of day I'd had; she already knew. I guess the entire school did.

"I'll bet you hated to walk back into Miss Twit's class after that," C.B. said, shifting her books to the other arm.

"I don't know what Mr. Pepper told her, except that she had to let me back in. She really has it in for me, C.B. And I haven't done anything to make her dislike me! I guess she thought, for a minute, that I'd fallen on something sharp and killed myself!"

C.B. giggled. "Did you look terrible?"

"Yeah." Now that it was all over, I could grin about it myself. "Well, it's done, that part of it. Let's go catch Killer."

And that's what we did.

We brought out the cat box—at the end of the yard, outside the fence, and screened from the house by the shrubbery—and I put the slices of liver in it. All but one, and that one I dangled between my fingers and offered to Killer, who was once again surveying the street from the low limb of that big tree.

He had his eyes wide open this time, and they were

fixed on that strip of liver. I doubted that the Caspitorian sisters could afford to feed all those cats much liver, but he knew what it was, all right.

C.B. stood beside me and talked to him. She knew how to talk to cats, not the off-hand, sort of rough way we did with Leroy, but in a soft, coaxing tone.

"Wouldn't you like some nice liver, Chester? See how good it looks? Come on, take a bite!"

She spoke to me without looking in my direction. "Give him that bit, Danny. Then show him where the rest of it is."

Cautiously, remembering how he'd scratched me the other time, I extended the liver until it dangled right in front of him.

I expected him to take it; but when he did, it was done so fast that I jerked back my hand and counted my fingers to see if they were all still there.

"He likes it," C.B. whispered, quite unnecessarily. "Now, let him see that there's more in the box."

And after a minute or so Killer leaped down from his tree limb and approached the box as he would have approached a mouse he intended to catch.

It was going to work, I thought. He was going to go in the box, and then I'd slam the top shut, and we'd have him.

He went in, all right, and I folded the top over as fast as I could, while C.B. crowed with delight.

Only it wasn't all downhill after that at all. Because as soon as he felt the lid closing over him, Killer forgot the liver and went wild.

I couldn't even hang onto the lid long enough to be worthwhile. The cat erupted out of the box as if he had been shot out of a cannon, right past my face and over my shoulder, leaving me feeling lucky to still have an ear.

"Oh, no! He got away!"

"I couldn't hold the lid down, he was stronger than I was." I stared after him, up into the tree where he'd disappeared among the leaves. And then I looked back at the box. The lid was torn right in two, where he'd pushed up and I'd pushed down. "Well, so much for that idea. He even got the liver, it's gone."

C.B. looked so disappointed I had to say something so she wouldn't know how bad I felt, too.

"Well, maybe I don't want to get into their old Secret Club, anyway. Anything that has Frankie for a leader can't be all that much fun."

"You're not giving up, are you? You still have a week and a half."

"Well, maybe," I said. "Maybe I'll think of something."

Only I sure didn't know what it would be.

All the rest of that week it rained. We didn't play ball, and I didn't think of any clever way to catch Killer. Finally C.B. and I went out to her garage and used some scraps of stuff her dad had to build another cage out of screen over a wooden frame. I nailed the screen between layers of wood so it wouldn't pull out easily, even with an angry twenty-pound cat in it, although when I remembered how hard Killer had pushed against me I wasn't sure *anything* would be strong enough.

"We'll have better luck this time," C.B. said, standing back to look at it when we'd finished.

"I hope so. Only I don't feel like going back there in the rain to try it. I hope it clears up before it's too late." I didn't mention my suspicions that Killer would be more wary the next time. Wary enough not to go into any kind of box, no matter what we put in it to tempt him.

Frankie knew what he was doing when he specified that it had to be Killer I caught. The other cats at the Caspitorian sisters' were friendly enough. We stopped in there on Thursday afternoon when Miss Rosie flagged us down from the porch.

We didn't see Killer, but Polly allowed me to pick her up and stroke her, and a dozen other cats wound around our feet when we went up to meet Miss Rosie.

"You're going to think I'm an awful old pest," she said. "You've been so kind, rescuing Roscoe, and everything. I hoped maybe you'd have some patience left for a pair of old ladies who aren't as spry as they used to be. We need something out of the attic, and we just aren't up to all of those stairs these days."

Before I could open my mouth, or even decide what I intended to say, C.B. said, "Sure, we'll get it for you. Just tell us what to do."

Well, I was just as curious as she was to see what was up there at the top of their house, so I nodded. "Sure. What is it you want us to bring down?"

We went into the house with her, cats curling around our ankles at every step. Miss Rosie scooped up a pair of kittens, a black one and a white one, and there seemed to be just as many as before still on the floor.

"It's a jewelry box we want," Miss Rosie said. Her

sister came into the hallway, rolling the chair along with her hands, and paused to listen without saying anything. "It belonged to our mother, and we haven't thought of it for years. We had all of her good jewelry, of course. This box just has some very old-fashioned things in it, not the kind we'd ever have worn ourselves. What's there isn't worth very much, I'm afraid, but Anna remembered it the other night, and we thought maybe we'd take the things out and see. Mr. Pritchard, who bought Papa's jewelry shop, will tell us if it's salable. Maybe for enough to get a new furnace, you see. It *might* be."

Her eyes, peering at us over the armful of kittens, were bright with hope.

We hadn't closed the door behind us, and the deep voice that came through the opening made us all jump.

"If you'd stop feeding all those fool cats and paying the vet bills on them, you'd have enough to maintain the place better."

It was Virgil Caspitorian, their nephew. I could tell from the way their mouths sort of went flat that neither of them welcomed him much.

Not that it seemed to bother him. He strode into the hallway, so that it felt pretty crowded, and he kicked out at one of the cats that got in his way.

Miss Rosie's eyes snapped in anger. "You have no call to be cruel to our pets, Virgil. If you don't like cats, I suggest that you not come inside. And I don't recall hearing you knock."

He ignored that. I looked past him and could see his wife sitting in the big car at the curb; I supposed she couldn't bear to come into the house with all these animals around.

"I came," their nephew said, "because a friend at the county clerk's office told me you haven't paid the second half of your taxes yet. Do you have the money to pay them?"

Miss Anna rolled her chair closer, and I saw that her knuckles were white on the wheels even after she came to a stop. "Your friend had no right to tell you anything about our taxes or our property. Those are confidential matters."

"Do you have the money to pay?" Virgil demanded. When neither of them answered right away, his face began to get red. "Don't you know that if you don't pay the taxes the county can eventually put the place up for sale? That someone will get it for practically nothing, just for paying the taxes, and that they'll throw you out of it?"

"They don't do that until the taxes are five years in arrears," Miss Annabel said. "Maybe by then we'll be dead and gone, and it won't matter to us, one way or the other."

It would matter to *him*, though, I thought. Was he afraid that if they sold the house for taxes *he* wouldn't get it? Did he think maybe he could find the money his grandfather had hidden, if the house belonged to him? Why didn't he offer to help them out and pay the taxes?

Then I remembered what Gramps had said about people who drive big cars and live in fancy houses, that those things aren't always paid for. Maybe Virgil Caspitorian wasn't as well off as he pretended to be.

The only thing for sure about him was that he was angry. He decided to drop the matter of the taxes for the moment. "What's this about needing a new furnace? Isn't the old one working?"

For a minute I thought they weren't going to answer that, either, and then Miss Rosie said, "We're having a few problems with it."

"You can't stay here through the winter if it isn't working," Virgil said. "You know that, don't you? You'd both die of pneumonia!"

All the talk about dying made me uncomfortable. I suppose I should have kept still, since none of this was really any of my business, but I felt as if I had to step in on the side of the old ladies.

"Maybe Gramps could take a look at your furnace. He's pretty good about fixing things," I said. "If he could fix it, then you wouldn't need a new one."

"That would be very kind of him," Miss Rosie said, although she didn't sound as if she had much hope he'd be able to do it. "And now, if that's all you came for, Virgil, you'll have to excuse us. We were about to transact some business."

She was so little, and he was so big, that it could have been funny seeing the two of them and watching Virgil back down. He gave me a look that clearly indicated he'd like to wring my neck. It was his aunts he spoke to, however.

"Make no mistake about this. If you're in such bad shape you can't pay the taxes or keep the place safe to live in, I'll have to follow my conscience and see that you're taken care of properly."

He had been holding his hat, which he now clamped firmly upon his head, and he marched out of the house, scattering cats ahead of him as he moved toward his car.

"He means to get us into a rest home, one way or another," Miss Rosie said, her face troubled as she watched Virgil climb into his car and drive away.

"Under the pretense that he's concerned about us," her sister agreed. "I can't imagine why. He'll inherit the house someday because he's the only relative we have left, but why would he *want* it? It's too big and too old-fashioned for him ever to want to live in it. I wonder if he overheard what you were saying to the children? About finding Mama's jewel box?"

"I hope not. I wouldn't want him to think there's anything valuable around here." Miss Rosie shook her head. "That's probably why he's interested in the house, though. He believes those old stories about the money Papa was supposed to have hidden here."

"You mean he didn't hide any?" C.B. asked. She sounded awfully disappointed.

The two old sisters looked at each other, and then Miss Rosie laughed.

"Oh, he did hide some, all right. We've found some of it, now and again. Nowhere near as much as people thought, though. Papa spent most of his money himself, I'm afraid. Poor Virgil! He's expecting so much, and he's going to get so little!"

"We don't have to leave the house to Virgil," Miss Anna said. "We could make out a will and leave it all to someone else."

Miss Rosie looked as if that had never occurred to her. She absentmindedly stroked the kitten she was still holding. "Who should we leave it to, then?"

Miss Anna hesitated, and then she said, "We could leave it to the cats! With someone to be their caretaker, of course."

They stared at each other, and then they both started to laugh. I'd never seen Miss Anna laugh before, and it changed her face so much she was like a different person.

Miss Rosie laughed hardest though, until she had to wipe her eyes. "Oh, my, wouldn't that make him furious! He doesn't like cats," she explained to us, as if we hadn't already been able to tell that. "He doesn't think we should waste any money on them. But the poor things, where would they be without us?"

"Well," C.B. said slowly, "maybe he's right that it's more important to have a new furnace than it is to . . . to put fancy collars on them. Things like that."

"Oh, the collars don't cost all that much. Mr. Katchourian sells those to us wholesale, you know, because he used to be a friend of Papa's. And we put the stones in ourselves. We learned how to do things like that when we used to help Papa," Miss Rosie explained. "I guess Anna would have been a jeweler herself, if girls had done things like that when **we** were young. She especially liked working with pretty things. And I think even a cat should be proud of itself, know it's important, don't you? A cat wearing a pretty collar doesn't feel like an unwanted stray, you see. No, I'm afraid Virgil simply has no heart when it comes to animals."

My personal opinion was that Virgil had no heart, period; naturally I didn't say so. I was more interested in getting on with the search for their mother's jewelry box.

"Oh, yes, let me see." Miss Rosie handed the kitten over to her sister and pulled a ring of keys out of her apron pocket. "Here. This one is marked *attic*. It opens the door at the foot of the stairs from the second floor up. They're all labeled, you see. This one to the east tower, and this one to west one, and this one to the north one, that's the square one."

"What's in the towers?" C.B. asked eagerly. By this time she had a cat in her arms, too; it was almost impossible, in this house, not to have a cat in your lap or your arms. Any cat except Killer, I thought.

"Not much of anything, as I recall," Miss Rosie said. "We haven't been up there in years, but I suspect it's all junk. Now, the jewelry box we want you to look for is about so big—" she measured with her hands—"and it's a black lacquered box, decorated in the Japanese style with a lovely scene. I can't remember exactly. There's a pagoda in it."

"What's a pagoda?" C.B. asked.

"Oh, it's one of their temple buildings, with a series of roofs with the edges turning up, like this." Again she gestured with her hands. "We don't know exactly where to tell you to look, but we think it's somewhere in the attic." She dropped the keys into my hands. "Do you want to start now?"

We did. We left our schoolbooks on the hall table, where they were immediately covered with cats. I hoped I'd been truthful when I told Virgil's wife that they were clean animals.

We went up the broad front stairway, seeing ourselves in the old mirror at the top (no ghosts on the landing, this time, because the window was closed and there were no curtains blowing), and then we went out of sight of the old ladies and climbed the rest of the way to the second floor.

We'd started up there fast enough. By the time we got to the top, we'd both slowed down quite a lot. Not only because it was a steep climb, and much higher stairs than either of us had at home, but because it was *different* up there.

C.B. stopped and looked around. "It's sort of spooky, isn't it?" Even her voice was slow and not much louder than a whisper.

It wasn't dark, only gloomy. There were windows at the far end of the hall, and some of the doors stood open, letting a little light into the upper hallway. I guessed the windows up here hadn't been washed in years, and the light they let in wasn't strong enough to keep deep shadows from forming in the corners.

It was dusty, too, dusty enough to make us both sneeze. I looked into the nearest bedroom and saw furniture draped in sheets and tattered curtains and more dust.

"I wonder if the lights work up here?" I flicked the switch, and a tiny pale bulb lit up. "It smells like mice, doesn't it?"

"I wouldn't think there'd be very many, not with all the cats around here. See, Polly's come with us! Where do you suppose the door to the attic stairs is?"

We found it after looking into a few more bedrooms. They were all pretty much alike, with faded wallpaper and pictures of people who must have been dead for a hundred years.

And then we came to a door that was locked. I put the key into the lock and turned it.

"Danny—look!" C.B. said. I took the key out of the lock and dropped the whole bunch into my pocket, then bent to look closer at what she was indicating. "Those look like new scratches, don't they?"

They sure did. Around the keyhole in that old dark metal were fresh, bright scratches. As if somebody had been poking around trying to get the door open without the key.

I heard C.B. swallow. "Someone's been up here."

"As long as they aren't up here now, what difference does it make?" I asked. I have to admit, though, that my heart was thumping in my chest when I opened the door.

There was nothing there. The dust looked as if it hadn't been disturbed in years.

"Whoever they were, they didn't get in," C.B. observed. "What do you think they wanted?"

"Easy. The whole town thinks old Mr. Caspitorian hid a fortune somewhere in the house. Anybody who could get in might have been looking for it."

"Virgil? I don't like Virgil. Do you think the ladies really found all of the money? Or might we come across some of it while we're looking for the jewelry box?"

We edged through the doorway and began to

climb the stairs, sneezing some more. Even Polly, at our heels, sneezed.

"They've probably looked everywhere. Still, there *might* be some they missed. It would be great if we found enough so they could replace their furnace and fix their roof, wouldn't it?"

"And pay their taxes," C.B. reminded me. Her voice sounded hollow, echoing between the walls of the stairway. She giggled suddenly, remembering. "Wouldn't it be funny if they did leave all the money to the cats?"

"It doesn't look to me as if there's much money to leave. You know, we ought to have a flashlight up here."

We had reached the top of the stairs and it was like being underwater, where the light doesn't reach. There were dirty windows at both ends of the enormous attic, but they filtered the sunlight so there wasn't much left of it by the time it reached the middle of the room.

"Oh, wow!" C.B. stopped and looked around. "What a neat place to explore! There must be a hundred years' worth of junk up here!"

"Yeah. It might make it hard to find one little black lacquered box, though."

After half an hour, I decided it wasn't even worth trying without more light. There were boxes and trunks and old furniture and a baby buggy with three wheels and stuff like that. And all of it was covered with so much dust we could hardly breathe.

Polly stayed with us, leaving little cat footprints across the tops of old tables and trunks. Sometimes she'd brush affectionately against us, and once she leaped onto my shoulder and teetered there, looking curiously into the box I was opening.

"She's trying to help," C.B. said, "only we aren't getting anywhere. There's so much stuff up here, that box could be anywhere. Like buried under a mountain of old clothes or inside one of those trunks. Is that one locked?"

I tried it, and the lid lifted with an eerie creaking sound that made me aware of the fading light and glad that I wasn't up there alone.

"Unlocked, and full of more junk. Do you think we have to look through everything in every one of these boxes? To see if the jewel box is at the bottom of one of them?"

C.B. sat back on her heels and brushed her hair off her forehead, leaving a dirty streak. "I think so. Only maybe we'd better come back to do it. With a flashlight or a lantern or something."

We'd been squatting so long one of my feet had gone to sleep, and I stamped it to get the circulation going again before we went downstairs. "OK. I think Gramps has a lantern. I guess they must have put the electricity in this house after it was built, or they'd have put at least a few lights in the attic."

We clattered down the stairs, and I took out the ring of keys. "Do you think they want this locked up again, or should we leave it open until we come back?"

C.B. paused and touched the scratch marks on the old black metal plate around the doorknob. "Someone tried to get in here, Danny. Maybe if we leave the place open, they'll come back and get into the attic. And whatever they want, I don't think they have a right to it, not even if it's Virgil Caspitorian."

She was right. I locked the door, and when we went back downstairs to confess we'd failed to find the jewelry box and I handed back the keys to Miss Rosie, I told her about the scratches around the lock.

She was, as usual, fondling a cat. She frowned a little. "Scratches? Perhaps they're old ones, though I don't remember them."

"They look fresh," C.B. said. "Has anybody been in your upstairs lately?"

"No. No, I don't think anyone's been up there in years, have they, Anna?"

"Maybe someone who visits you went up there without asking you," I suggested.

"I shouldn't think so. We don't have much company. The minister, once in a while. Virgil and his wife come about once a month, for a few minutes at a time, but they've never gone upstairs. And the Holmans have been in the kitchen occasionally. They have a garden, and they bring over vegetables. They've been especially helpful lately, although I keep assuring them we don't really need any help. And you two." She smiled a warm, sweet smile, and I thought if the other kids could see her, they wouldn't think she was peculiar, any more than their own grandmothers were. "You don't know how much we've enjoyed having a couple of young people in. No, I don't think anyone's been upstairs for years."

I didn't argue. What was the use?

But as went down the path to the front gate, I remembered that face I'd seen in the tower window. Either it was a ghost or someone had found a way to get inside the Caspitorian house.

9

We didn't get back to the Cat Ladies' house until Saturday morning. On Friday it rained sheets, and Mrs. Hope came to pick us up after school. C.B. asked if she couldn't drop us off at the Caspitorians' and come back for us later, only her mother said she didn't want to come out again in such bad weather, didn't want C.B. to walk home in the rain, and thought that jeans would be more appropriate to wear in a dirty attic than the skirt and blouse C.B. had on.

So we went on home, where I discovered Leroy was in trouble again. Somehow he'd accidentally been left inside (probably in my bedroom) when Aunt Mattie went out, leaving meat to defrost on the kitchen counter. Gramps had been playing cards with his friend Teddy Bear (no kidding, that's really his name), so with no one to say, "no," Leroy helped himself to the hamburger we were supposed to have for supper.

By the time I got there, right behind Gramps, Leroy was lying with his nose between his paws in the corner, and Aunt Mattie was stumping around angrily muttering to herself.

It didn't seem like a good time to talk to anybody about anything, so I went to my room and did my homework. It wasn't until after supper, which turned out to be macaroni and cheese instead of meatloaf, that I got a chance to mention the Cat Ladies' furnace to Gramps and tell him about the jewel box.

"Maybe I shouldn't have suggested you'd look at their furnace," I said. "Only that nephew of theirs made me so mad . . ."

"Has that effect on people, doesn't he?" Gramps agreed. "Well, if you kids are going back there tomorrow to look for that jewel box, I'll tag along and look at the furnace. You going to stay all day?"

Remembering the quantity of junk in that attic, I nodded. "I guess so. Maybe we'll take a lunch and make it a picnic."

So that's what we did. I had liverwurst and cheese sandwiches and C.B. brought apple fritters rolled in sugar; we each ate one on the way to town, while they were still warm. She'd brought some for Gramps, too.

Leroy looked at us mournfully when we left. The

skies had cleared so we didn't mind walking, and that big old ugly dog sat in the pen Gramps had made for him and whimpered when we turned away.

When we got there, Miss Rosie gave us the keys and we went on upstairs while Gramps headed for the basement. We could hear the two of them chattering away as we climbed the stairs. I thought Miss Rosie sounded happy to have all this company in her house.

We had a lantern, this time. Gramps had showed me how to handle it, and I'd promised not to let it get knocked over. We found a protruding nail to hang it on, and it was almost as good as an electric light.

Not that it helped us find what we were after. We went through boxes of papers and old photographs, the drawers of a desk that had one corner propped up with books because it had lost a leg, and containers of clothes that looked as if somebody'd been saving them for a hundred years.

"They'd make great costumes, if we wanted to put on a play," C.B. said, holding up a red satin dress with a long, full skirt.

We didn't find the jewel box. We did learn, though, just about the time we decided to take a lunch break, that we had unexpected company.

Polly was there; she'd followed us up the same as she had the first time. And when I sat down Indian-fashion and brushed the dust off my hands before I

dug into the sack for a sandwich, I saw that Polly had a visitor.

Excitement prickled through me. For there was Killer, sitting at the head of the stairs, a black silhouette against the dim light from below. C.B. saw him at the same time I did. I heard her suck in her breath. "Don't pay any attention to him," I said. "Pretend we don't see him."

"How are you going to make friends with him that way?"

"Maybe we'll have to let *him* make friends with *us*. I wonder if he'd like liverwurst? I'll put some down here and see if he's interested."

Polly was; she came sniffing delicately around the bit of sandwich and then ate it.

Killer made no move. He just watched us with those slitted amber eyes.

Half my time was gone already. If I didn't manage to take Killer to some member of the Secret Club by the following Saturday, I was out of luck. Permanently barred from the club.

So I caught Polly and held her, stroking her and talking to her, and C.B. put out another bit of liverwurst sandwich.

Killer stayed where he was. I wondered if he'd have been more trusting if we hadn't tried to stuff him into a box a few days earlier.

Neither one of us saw him sneak up, finally, and

get the food. We went ahead with eating our lunch and talking, and all of a sudden we noticed that Killer was gone. So was the sandwich.

"He did like it! Danny, maybe if we keep coming back and feeding him, you can win him over yet!"

"Maybe," I said. "Listen, let's go downstairs and see how Gramps is coming with the furnace before we start looking again, OK? There isn't that much more in the way of places to look. We've gone through everything but that one corner, haven't we? Two more trunks and four or five boxes."

We didn't see anything of Killer when we went downstairs. He must have been the only one of the thirty-two or thirty-three cats that wasn't in the house, judging by the number of them milling around. We realized why they were all there when Polly leaped out of my arms and ran across the kitchen to the feeding dishes. Miss Rosie had just put out their food.

"Poor babies. I usually feed them right after break-fast," she told us. "This morning I forgot because I was down in the cellar with Mr. Minden. And do you know, he thinks he can fix it? I got so excited I didn't think about anything else at all!"

"I'm glad somebody's having some luck," C.B. said. "We haven't had any yet. We should finish with the attic by this afternoon. What if we don't find the jewel box in those last few boxes?"

"Well, I suppose it's possible that the box was left in one of the rooms on the second floor, although I wouldn't have thought so. You can try the other rooms, though most of them haven't much left in them anymore."

I couldn't help thinking about that face I'd seen in the upper window. I didn't believe it was a ghost, and I knew it hadn't been either of the Caspitorian sisters. Somebody else had figured out a way to get into the house, I decided, somebody who didn't belong there at all. They didn't have keys, but they were looking for something valuable, and maybe they'd already found the jewel box.

Still, I didn't *know* that. And the longer I hung around the house, the more likely it seemed that I might win over Killer, at least enough to get him into the new cage we'd constructed for him.

I felt guilty thinking about that cage, though. I was pretty sure Miss Rosie would be horrified at the thought of anybody putting one of her precious pets into a cage for any reason at all. Certainly she wouldn't approve of doing anything by force, and probably that was the only way I'd ever get Killer. He wasn't like Polly, who liked to be held and petted.

I went down and talked to Gramps for a few minutes. He had the burner out of the furnace and looked dirtier than we did. He grinned at me happily.

"Take me a few hours to get this cleaned up and put it back in, and then I bet it'll work, all right. It's just clogged up, looks like. It's an old furnace and I don't know if they could get a new burner for it, but this one's not worn out yet. Won't that Virgil be pleased?"

We both laughed, and so did Miss Rosie, who had followed me down the stairs.

"Poor Virgil," she said. "He never was one of my favorite people, even when he was a little boy. He always had to have his own way about everything, or he sulked. I can't bear people who sulk, especially after they're grown-up. Do you really think it's going to work, Mr. Minden?"

Gramps had a slender file he was using to scrape the rust or whatever it was out of the holes in the burner. He nodded. "Yep. I think so. And I remember when you used to call me *Charlie*."

"I guess I did, didn't I? All right, Charlie. Do you mind if I watch you, if I don't talk too much? Anna says I talk too much."

"Have the same problem myself," Gramps said cheerfully. "Maybe we can get some of it out of our systems, talking to each other."

They didn't need me. I could see that. I went back up to the kitchen, where C.B. was talking to Miss Anna. She looked troubled, and when we were out of Miss Anna's hearing she told me why.

1 2 1

"I think they really need the money pretty badly, Danny. She said the price of cat food was going up so much she hoped no more cats would come around and need to be taken care of. She even said they'd tried to find other homes for some of them, but Indian Lake is such a small town and practically everybody already has cats. And they can't just turn them out, the way *some* people do with their pets when they get tired of taking care of them. I think I'll ask Mom if I can have one of the kittens; Miss Anna said I could if I wanted it. How about your aunt? Do you think she'd take a kitten?"

"She isn't very happy about our having Leroy. Can you imagine Leroy and a cat in the same house?" I shook my head. "I don't think that would work. It'll be easier to find that jewelry box for them than to talk Aunt Mattie into another animal."

"All right. Let's go find the jewel box, then."

We went through the rest of the stuff in the attic that afternoon, and except for a stack of old *National Geographics* that had some pictures nearly as good as the ones my dad takes, we didn't find anything interesting. Certainly not the jewel box.

C.B. sat in the dust with slumped shoulders, her mouth drooping. "It's not here. It couldn't be, or we'd have found it."

"In a house the size of this one, there are still plenty of places it could be," I said. "They admit they haven't seen it in years and don't remember anything about it. Anyway, I want to see what's in the towers, don't you?"

She sat up straighter. "Where was the window where you saw the face?"

"In the square tower." I looked at the ring of keys Miss Rosie had given me, squinting to read the labels on them. "There are keys for each tower. Let's go see them."

C.B. got to her feet, wiping her hands on her jeans. "What if whoever it was is still there?"

"What do you think? That they've got a demented relative chained up in the tower?"

"What's *demented?*"

"Crazy. Somebody who has to be locked up for his own good. You know."

"Oh. Well, no, in a town the size of Indian Lake I don't think they could have anybody around for long without the neighbors finding out about it. And if they *did*, someone would have to come up here to feed them and everything, wouldn't they? And neither of them can climb the stairs. Come on, let's go."

I was convinced that the Cat Ladies didn't come upstairs any more. But there *had* been someone up here recently; I was sure of that. So I did feel sort of funny when we found the door to the square tower, and there were the same scratch marks around the lock. Only this door was unlocked.

We stood there for a minute, looking at the dust on the stairs. Because this time, there were tracks in it.

Oh, they weren't good footprints, so that we could tell the size and shape of the shoes or anything like that. In fact, it looked to me as if someone had gone up and down more than a few times recently, too many times to provide anything in the way of clues.

We looked at each other, and then I led the way up the little stairway, because although the door to the tower was on the second floor, the tower itself stuck up on a level with the attic, but separate from it.

It was a terrific room, when we got there. We guessed at once that this was the tower where old Mr. Caspitorian had spent his final days, because there was still a bed and a lot of dusty furniture. It didn't even have sheets over it, the way the stuff did on the lower floor.

And it had a view. There were windows on three sides of it, and from there we could see from the lake on one side, out over all the neighboring houses, over to the school grounds on the other side. I could even see some kids on the school grounds playing ball, though I couldn't make out who they were from that distance.

C.B. forgot she'd been apprehensive about there being someone up here. She stood at the window, looking down into the side yard.

"Wow! I'd sure like to have a room like this, wouldn't you?"

"Yeah. I'd like some different furniture, though. And the roof leaks; the wallpaper's peeling off the ceiling."

Her tone changed. "Danny. Come here."

"What?" My toe caught in a hole in the rug and I nearly fell into the window.

"Isn't that the next door neighbor? What's his name, Mr. Holman? What's he doing in this back yard?"

It was him, all right. There couldn't be two heads of fuzzy hair like that, with a bald spot in the middle. He had his back to us, and he was standing alongside the barrel Miss Rosie used to burn trash. We couldn't tell what he was doing.

Not until he moved away, and then I saw that he carried a small red can in one hand. He walked quickly to the back of the house and disappeared under the trees.

A red can? The only thing I ever knew people to have in a red can was gasoline.

For a minute I forgot that C.B. was there, and that we were supposed to be looking for a jewelry box.

C.B. said something I didn't hear. I was remembering how Miss Rosie had dropped a lighted match into the papers she was burning and how the fire had flared up and scorched her hair and burned her hands before she could get out of the way. She said she hadn't put anything like gasoline into the barrel.

Maybe someone else had, though.

Why on earth would Mr. Holman do that? He pretended to be concerned about the old ladies, had offered to help them with chores. I couldn't see how pouring gas in their trash barrel would be of any help, especially if he neglected to tell them he'd done it.

In fact, the only reason I could think of why he'd do such a thing was to cause trouble. To scare Miss Rosie, or make it look as if she were irresponsible.

It was a nasty thought.

I told C.B. what I was thinking. And she didn't tell me it was silly. She looked as troubled as I felt.

"Why would he want to do that? Frighten her, or hurt her?"

I wasn't quite sure, except that I suspected it had something to do with the money that was supposed to be hidden in this house.

"Remember how Miss Rosie said Mrs. Holman offered to do their housework? For pay, of course. Maybe that was just an excuse to try to get inside the house."

"Uh-huh. Only I don't quite see how making it dangerous for Miss Rosie to burn trash would help them get into the house."

I didn't quite see, either, but my instinctive dislike for the Holmans deepened. I'd have to think about this.

C.B. had turned away from the window and was examining a heavy china pitcher and basin on the dresser. "Look at this. They must have had to carry all the water up and down the stairs while Mr. Caspitorian was sick up here. I'm glad I wasn't the one taking care of him."

"Seems like this room would be where he hid the money, if this is where he stayed most of the time. Do you suppose there's a secret compartment or hidden room somewhere? If he built the house, there might be, and he'd know where it was."

We went around poking walls and peeled back the rug to look at the floor, hoping for something like that. We didn't find a thing. There were a few odds and ends left in the dresser drawers, but nothing of any value.

We both felt pretty let down, not finding anything after all that work. We went down to the second floor and were just figuring out where the door to one of the round towers would be when we heard a terrible racket. Someone cried out, and then there was nothing but silence.

C.B. and I looked at each other for a few seconds, then raced for the stairs, dreading what we'd find.

10

Miss Anna had rolled her chair to the back door onto the rear enclosed porch and was calling out anxiously. "Rosie? Rosie, are you all right?"

Gramps got there about the same time we did. He was the first one out the door, and C.B. and I were right behind him.

Miss Rosie hadn't answered her sister. We saw why right away. The old lady was sprawled under what had been a big stack of wood cut for the kitchen stove. She didn't move until after we'd all gotten down on our hands and knees to lift the wood off from her. Then Gramps touched her wrist to see if she still had a pulse.

"Rosie, can you hear me?"

Miss Rosie groaned. "Oh, my! I feel as if I've been run over by a truck!" She pushed herself into a sitting position, and we could actually watch the bruises form purple spots on her face and arms.

Gramps pitched one more stick of wood off to the side. "How the heck did you manage to knock all that over on yourself?" he asked.

She looked up at what was left of the winter wood supply stacked against the wall at one end of the big glassed-in porch. "All I did was reach up to get a few chunks, and the top board of the rack that holds them in place came off. They all fell on me."

We helped her up, and she hobbled into the kitchen. Gramps paused long enough to look at the boards that had been nailed to the framework of the rack that held the firewood in place. "Looks like the nails just pulled out. I'll get a hammer and fix it."

"Never had anything like that happen before," Miss Rosie said, leaning against the table and accepting the cup of tea that her sister brought for her. "Maybe Virgil is right. Maybe this place is getting dangerous for a couple of old women. Maybe we're getting too old to stay alone."

I didn't say anything. I was sure thinking fast, though. I thought about how much Virgil Caspitorian wanted his aunts in a rest home, and I was suspicious enough to wonder if maybe he'd do something to help them get there. Like arrange for accidents to happen.

I almost asked Gramps, when he came into the kitchen after replacing the boards and picking up the firewood, if it looked as if somebody could have pulled the nails out so that sooner or later the pressure of the wood would make the board fail.

I didn't, though, because it isn't the kind of thing you say in front of the person who's just been the victim. And besides, Gramps didn't give me much of an opportunity to say anything to him.

"I got the wood back where it belongs, and it'll hold all right, now. I brought in a few chunks to use tonight." He dumped them into the box beside the stove. "I got that burner back in. I'll go down and light it off, see how it does. You let me know if the heat starts coming up through the registers, OK?"

Miss Rosie drank her tea. She was so shaken, and so bruised, that Miss Anna thought maybe they ought to call the doctor.

"No, no," she protested. "No need to get him out. I'm all right. Except that I'm going to be black and blue all over. I think I will lie down for a bit, though."

A few minutes later, C.B. gave a triumphant cry. "There's heat, I can feel it! Mr. Minden fixed the furnace!" She smiled broadly at Miss Anna. "So you won't have to have a new one, after all." Then, the smile fading, she added, "We didn't find the jewelry box in the attic or in the square tower. Do you want us to keep looking?"

Miss Anna sighed. I thought she looked almost as shaken as Miss Rosie, and no wonder. If something happened to her sister, there was no question but what she'd have to leave her home. She couldn't take care of herself alone, even if she did manage to do a lot more things than you'd expect.

"Well, I guess you've spent enough time here today. When you get a chance, though, maybe you'll come back. It has to be up there somewhere."

Then she looked at our faces and saw how we felt about it. She made a little grunting sound. "Oh, don't feel sorry for us! We don't tell Virgil everything; we still have some resources he doesn't know about. We're rather careful, of course. Papa lived to be ninety-six, and our whole family runs to ripe old ages. We may have another twenty or thirty years to support ourselves, so we don't waste anything. If that old jewelry of Mama's doesn't show up, we won't have to go off to the home the way Virgil hopes we will. It would just be easier to convert the jewelry into cash than"—she hesitated over the word—"than converting other valuables would be. And if the furnace works now, that'll save us a lot. We certainly thank you, all of you."

So we left, and probably I should have told Gramps what I was thinking, but I didn't.

Half my time was gone for catching Killer. Maybe I could still do it, though. I'd come back and look some more for the jewel box, and while I was doing that I'd leave tidbits around for that cat. Maybe by *next* Saturday I could entice him into letting me touch him. Maybe.

"Danny! Danny, wake up, boy!"

Gramps was shaking my shoulder, and I reared up on my elbows, coming out of a dream where I was facing Killer bare-handed, only he was twenty times his real size, and he was going to tear me to pieces.

"Huh? What's the matter?" I could hardly remember where I was for a minute, and then I realized it was Sunday morning. "Oh, church. Am I late?"

"No. We just got an emergency," Gramps said. "A message from Anna Caspitorian, wants us to hightail it up there to their house, you and me. Ben Newton just brought the message, and he'll give us a ride, if you'll get a hustle on."

I slid out of bed, still fighting sleep, so I banged into the corner of the dresser, and wondering what the emergency was. Ben Newton is the sheriff, so I hoped it wasn't anything serious.

I was still smoothing down my hair when I went out into the kitchen where the sheriff and Gramps were each having a cup of coffee.

"What's wrong?" I wanted to know.

Ben Newton finished his cup and put it down on the drainboard. "Well, I guess you were there yesterday when Miss Rosie had an accident, had that woodpile fall on her and knock her down."

"She wasn't hurt bad, though," I said, forgetting about my hair.

"Well, didn't seem so at the time. But she's bruised and sore all over, and she has a heart problem, you know. Her nephew asked me to check on the old ladies from time to time, and just on a hunch I thought maybe I'd ought to do it this morning. Maybe it wasn't a hunch, there just wasn't any smoke coming out of their kitchen chimney the way there usually is when I go to work, so I pulled in and waded through the cats and rang the bell."

He wasn't standing around, we were hustling out the door and toward the police car parked in the driveway while he talked. I crawled in the front beside Ben, and Gramps squeezed in on my other side.

"It was Miss Anna came to the door, in her wheel-chair. She'd been trying to get the fire going, all right, because Miss Rosie wasn't feeling well enough to get up." Ben backed expertly and headed the police car toward town. "So we talked to her, and both of us felt she ought to see the doctor. I hung around until he came over, and he decided she should check into the hospital for a few days for some tests and x-rays. Well, Miss Rosie refused to go, at first. Said she couldn't leave Anna alone, which is true, of course."

Just what Virgil wanted, I thought. If Miss Rosie went to the hospital, Miss Anna would wind up in a rest home. And not only would the two of them be out of the house, but he could probably get keys to it so he could have the run of the place. Was that what he wanted? Was that why he'd asked the sheriff to keep an eye on his aunts, knowing that sooner or later this would happen? Or had he even helped it happen, somehow? Like pulling those boards off so that if Miss Rosie unbalanced the firewood some of it would fall on her?

I thought all that in between what the sheriff and Gramps were saying.

"So," Ben Newton went on, "I finally suggested that they get someone to come in and stay with Miss Anna for a few days, and you're the one they wanted, son."

I'd been wondering what my part was in all this, and I sat up straighter. "Me?" I sounded squeaky. "You mean, they want me to stay with Miss Anna while her sister is in the hospital?"

"That's what they said. Seems Miss Anna can get out of bed and into her chair by herself, and do most things, except get up and down stairs. She can't run errands, and with no phone in that house, she'd be too cut off from everyone to be safe, all by herself. But Miss Rosie thinks you're reliable and that you can handle everything. How about that? How do you think she got the idea Danny's reliable, eh, Charlie?"

Gramps just chuckled.

I was feeling sort of peculiar. I wondered if Gramps would be amused if he knew about that face I'd seen in the tower window, and Mr. Holman carrying a gas can around in the Cat Ladies' back yard, and the scratch marks around the locks and the footprints in the dust in places where there weren't supposed to be any people. Not to mention the way that board had pulled loose and let the firewood fall on Miss Rosie.

"I don't reckon Danny's afraid to stay there for a few days, are you, Danny?" Gramps asked.

It was like I was hollow inside. If I told him, now, about all those things, would both of them think it was because I was a coward? I swallowed hard. "What will I have to do? I mean, I can't stay there every day, because I have to go to school."

"Oh, just be there at night, see that Miss Anna has a fire before you leave in the morning, that wood's brought in to last through the day, pick up their mail and bring it in, take out the trash for her, that kind of thing."

Neither of them noticed that I didn't answer. Ben pulled up in front of the old castlelike house, and we all piled out. I knew if I *wasn't* going to stay there, I'd better say so at once. Only my throat sort of closed and I couldn't seem to say anything.

And then I saw Miss Rosie, and I knew I couldn't refuse to help her. There was a terrible purple mark on one side of her face, and bruises on her arms, too. And I could tell by looking at her that she didn't feel well at all, even if she did say it was silly to want her to go to the hospital.

She gave me a feeble smile. "Danny, how nice of you to come. I know I won't be gone long, and Anna can manage just about everything if there's someone here to help a little bit. Otherwise, I'm afraid Virgil will rush in and whisk us both off to a rest home before we know what's going on."

So, what could I do? I agreed to stay.

"I'll bring you some clothes and stuff after church," Gramps said. He rumpled my hair, laughing. "What this boy will do to get out of going to church!"

The doctor, who was standing around looking anxious, patted me on the shoulder. "Good boy. We shouldn't have to keep Miss Rosie in the hospital more than a week—maybe less than that."

A week! I swallowed again, but nobody was paying any attention to me by this time. They were more interested in getting Miss Rosie ready to leave. They all went out in a group, Miss Rosie with the doctor, and Gramps with the sheriff, leaving me with Miss Anna.

I'd have felt comfortable with Miss Rosie. I didn't feel at all at ease with Miss Anna. I couldn't tell if the expression on her face was because she didn't like me or because her arthritis was hurting her.

I offered to bring in some wood for the stove, and then she cooked breakfast for us once the fire got hot enough. I wondered how she could tell when it was right; all the cook stoves I ever saw had a way to turn the heat up and down, but this one didn't. You just stuck wood into it and poked it with an iron poker, though I wasn't sure what *that* did.

She made a good breakfast, though. I watched, and I began to get the idea. When you wanted a lot of heat, you put the pan out in the middle. If you wanted it low, for scrambled eggs, you put it off to the side.

We didn't talk much during the meal, and afterward I wondered if I should offer to do the dishes. I hate doing dishes, though, and I was glad when she started running water in the sink and said over her shoulder, "I can do these without help. Maybe you'd like to take the keys and look around upstairs again, see if you can find that box of Mama's trinkets. Oh, and you'll need a key to the outside doors, too. They're hanging on a nail just inside the back door, out there on the back porch."

Only they weren't. Or, rather, there were some keys there, but not one to the back door.

Miss Anna looked down at the ring of keys I'd brought her, frowning. "That's odd. Why would anyone have taken the key to the back door?"

My peculiar feeling was coming back. "Do you use those keys very much?" I asked.

"No. Rosie has another set. These used to be mine, when I could still get around. Since I haven't needed them, we let them hang there on the nail." She flipped through them again, looking at the labels that said what they were keys to. "I don't see how that one key could have come off if none of the others did."

I did. That nail was right inside the back door, where anybody could walk up when he knew the old ladies weren't looking and help himself. With them labeled the way they were, he wouldn't have to waste much time getting the right one.

And once somebody—I didn't say who—had that key, he could get into the house and look for whatever he was looking for, even when the Cat Ladies thought they were securely locked inside.

I didn't say anything about it, though. We found Miss Rosie's key ring, and Miss Anna said I was to keep that as long as I stayed.

As long as I stayed. The hollow feeling was getting worse, and I didn't know what to do about it. I had a strong idea that I ought to have told Gramps and maybe Ben Newton the things I suspected.

Only they were gone, and there was no phone. I could walk over to the sheriff's office, I guessed, but something held me back from doing that.

One of the things was that Miss Anna asked if I'd feed the cats.

The cat food was bought in fifty pound sacks and then dumped into some big plastic garbage cans in the pantry off the kitchen. A man delivered them and did the dumping because they were too heavy for Miss Rosie to handle.

All the cats were there, rubbing against my ankles and making mewing sounds while I dished out the cat food. Even Killer.

Not that *he* rubbed against my ankles. He stayed well back, watching from a windowsill, but he was there.

I figured if I stayed in the house for a week—the

last week I had to produce Killer to win my way into the Secret Club—there was at least a small chance that I could do it.

Anyway, I put out food for all of them, and Killer crept up and got his after I was well away from the dishes. Cautious, that was Killer. Still, he was a smart cat. I was sure he knew who fed him.

OK, then. I'd stay in the house until Miss Rosie came home, and I'd try to win over old Killer.

I made up my mind not to think about that face in the tower window, or the fact that I was sure somebody had a key to the back door. I didn't think about those things—much—until after it got dark that night.

11

C.B. showed up in the middle of that Sunday after-noon. She'd found out from Aunt Mattie where I was, and she came to help me with more searching in the upstairs. Her green eyes were all sparkly; she thought it was a terrific opportunity.

"Especially if you're feeding Killer every day," she said.

"Sure," I agreed and told her about the key to the back door.

"Well, prop a chair under the doorknob or some-thing, so they can't get in even with their key," she said.

I stared at her. I'd expected a little more concern than that. "And what if the chair doesn't hold? What if he gets in anyway?"

"Well, he isn't trying to hurt anybody, is he? He's

looking for that money Old Man Caspitorian hid."

"How do we know he won't hurt anybody?"

"He never hurt *them*, did he? And he's a human being, not a ghost, the way the kids think. I'd rather face a human being than a ghost."

I wasn't sure about that. It depended on how mean the human being was, and I thought that anybody who would deliberately try to arrange fake accidents for old ladies was pretty mean. I had never met any ghosts, so I didn't know about *them*.

We didn't meet any ghosts in the towers and the second floor rooms that afternoon, either. But we saw signs that someone had been in some of them.

Footprints in the dust—again too messed up to tell the size or shape—and drawers pulled out of dressers, and closet doors left standing open. We could tell they hadn't been that way all along, because they were less dusty than the rooms themselves.

We did have one advantage over the mysterious intruder, though. We had keys to the locked rooms. And after I looked at the key ring on the nail near the back door, I figured out why he didn't have them —or, rather, I asked Miss Anna, and she told me. There was only one complete set of keys that included those for the towers, and that was on Miss Rosie's key ring.

"Papa had keys for all the rooms, once. But we didn't used to keep them locked. I don't know why we keep them locked now, except," Miss Anna said with a wry smile, "we suspected that when Virgil and Eleanor came to visit, one of them might sneak off and snoop around. *He* would, anyway, on the pretext of making sure everything was all right. We told him we'd already found what little Papa left, but I don't think he believes us."

"But can you be positive you actually have found *all* of it?" C.B. asked. "Maybe there's still some of it hidden somewhere."

"We found it," Miss Anna said, and something about her voice made me think she really believed they had. I couldn't help wondering what they'd done with it, if there really was quite a bit. They certainly didn't appear to have spent much on their house or themselves. Virgil was angry because of what they spent on the cats, but even with more than thirty cats they couldn't have spent a fortune on food, vet bills, and collars bought wholesale and trimmed by hand.

We did have some good luck at last, though. Or maybe it wasn't luck, after all; Miss Anna remembered something.

We'd been downstairs for cookies and milk. Miss Anna was baking more cookies because she said she had to do something to keep herself busy, and today it was peanut butter ones. The smell drifted up the stairway until it lured us down to the kitchen.

"It's the kind of house," C.B. suggested, "that

looks as if it would have secret stairways, or rooms, or something."

Miss Anna shook her head. "No. Nothing like that. Although, come to think of it, there was a secret compartment."

We both must have looked excited because she put up her hands in protest. "No, no. Not really. We only called it that, when we were children. It was actually only a storage area under the attic stairs. It opens off that front bedroom, which is where Rosie used to sleep when she was a girl. I'd forgotten all about it. We haven't used it in a long time. There's just a chance, though, that we might have put Mama's jewel box in there. We weren't hiding it, we simply stored things there, and the box might have been among those things. You can take a look."

We'd have run right up there, in mid-cookie, only she stopped us to explain how to open the compartment.

After that, we didn't waste any time.

It had been a pretty room once, I guess. Now the wallpaper was so faded the flowers looked brown instead of pink, and the dust was as thick as everywhere else.

We'd never have found the hidden compartment if Miss Anna hadn't remembered it. It was just a part of the wall, and there was a chair in front of it. When we moved the chair aside, the upholstery material on the chair ripped just from our taking hold of it.

But behind the chair, there was the wooden panel, just as Miss Anna had said. Actually, the whole bottom part of the room was paneled in dark wood, and the wood was in sections like picture frames, only without pictures; the middles were smooth panels of wood.

One of the sections was hinged, with hinges painted the color of the paneling so they didn't show even when you got close to them. We felt around for the edge opposite the hinges, and a moment later we were looking into the compartment.

It was big enough for a person to crawl into, although neither of us could have stood up in it. And there, with some more boxes of old photographs and some magazines printed about forty years ago, we found a box.

For a minute we were sure we had found what we'd been looking for because it was black and it was the right size. When C.B. opened it, though, it didn't have any jewelry in it. It had a bunch of little tiny tools, like files and a drill and some other stuff neither of us recognized.

"Darn," C.B. said, and she put all of her disappointment into the word.

"Well, it's not quite like the box they described to us," I said. "So let's keep on hunting."

And then, only a few minutes later, we found

another box under a photograph album that practically came apart in my hands. I didn't pay any attention to that, though, because *this* box wasn't plain like the first one.

I brushed the dust off and saw the gleam of black lacquer and the tiny scarlet pagoda; I gave a cry of triumph. "This is it! We found it!"

We carried it downstairs to Miss Anna. She set it on her lap and we held our breaths when she opened it.

The stuff in it was pretty. "Old-fashioned," Miss Anna said and showed us two rings. One of the stones looked like a ruby, but she said it was a garnet. There were several brooches, those pins ladies used to wear on their dress fronts, and a necklace that came apart, the string rotted, when she picked it up, so that the beads fell all over the box and her lap.

And there were three or four pair of earrings. "Junk," Miss Anna said. "Most of it. Nobody wears brooches any more, but some of the stones might be worth putting into a new setting." She closed the box and handed it to me. "Maybe you could take it to Mr. Pritchard after school tomorrow and ask if any of it's worth selling."

I nodded. "OK."

"We found this, too." C.B. offered the first box with the tiny tools to Miss Anna. "What are these things for?"

"Oh, mercy. So that's where it got to." Miss Ann opened the box and looked at its contents. "Those are Papa's tools. I have some, too, because I helped him once in a while, but these were his own, the ones he worked with here at home. Did Rosie tell you Papa was a jeweler? He made lovely things." She stuck out one of her stiff hands, and we saw the ring there, a heavy silver one with a milky stone with pale colors in it that changed with the light as she moved. "This one is an opal; he made the ring for me for my twentieth birthday. I guess you think it's silly, an old woman like me, wearing something like this."

"No," I said. "Why should it be silly? It's pretty enough so anybody'd want to wear it, I should think. We thought we'd found the jewelry box when we found this one. It was disappointing when it only had tools in it."

"Well. I guess our mission is accomplished. I might as well go home," C.B. said. She looked at me over Miss Anna's head, and I could tell she thought the *real* mission, capturing Killer, was going to be resolved satisfactorily, too.

I walked with her to the front door. It was too bad she wasn't a boy, I thought; if she were, I'd ask her to stay here with me until Miss Rosie came home. It would make a lot of difference, having someone besides Miss Anna in the house.

C.B. was thinking about that, too. "You going to

sleep in one of the towers?" she asked.

"I don't know yet where I'm going to sleep. Wherever Miss Anna says, I suppose."

"I'd sleep in the tower," C.B. said, with all the courage of a person who wasn't going to have to do it. "Maybe that way you'd find out who it is who gets into the house."

I wasn't sure I wanted to know, if I had to find out by having them walk into the room where I was sleeping, and I said so.

"You're not scared of staying here, are you, Danny?"

I managed to sound scornful, as if the idea was absurd. "Heck, no! What is there to be scared of?"

I felt peculiar again when she'd gone, though.

Miss Anna tried to make me feel welcome, even though she wasn't used to having anyone to be hospitable to. We were eating supper—she wasn't as good a cook as Aunt Mattie, but she was pretty good with chicken and dumplings—when there was a knock on the back door.

It wasn't locked, of course. Nobody ever locked their doors in the daytime in Indian Lake. And the next door neighbors walked right on in.

Mrs. Holman called, "Hoo-hoo, Miss Anna?"

"Come in," Miss Anna said.

The Holmans crossed the porch and entered the

kitchen, stopping with narrowed eyes when they saw me.

It was the first time I'd been close to Mrs. Holman. She had a lot of freckles to go with her red hair, and though she was smiling, I didn't think the smile went any deeper than Virgil's wife's smile did.

"Don't get up, go on with your meal while it's hot," she said. "We were concerned; we'd been out for a ride and when we got back we found out your sister's gone to the hospital."

"Just for some tests," Anna said.

"Overnight, though? Maybe for several days? You can't stay here alone, Miss Anna. I'll be happy to come over and keep you company."

"I have company. Danny's here," Miss Anna said. "So I'm not alone."

Mrs. Holman laughed. Her husband, standing behind her, didn't look as if he thought it was funny. "He's only a boy, a child!"

"I'm eleven," I said, and the peculiar feeling got worse, almost enough to spoil my appetite.

"Well, *eleven*. Seriously, Miss Anna, I insist on staying with you. So there'll be an adult in the house, in case you need anything."

"Danny can do anything for me that I need done. There isn't much, you know. Except for taking out the trash and carrying in wood, I can do everything as well as Rosie does it. She cleaned house only a few days ago, and Danny can feed the cats, so there won't be anything special to do before Rosie comes home. I appreciate your thinking of me, though."

Mrs. Holman licked her lips uncertainly, then glanced at her husband. I couldn't tell what his look meant, but I guess she knew.

"Well, to make me feel better, let me stay tonight. I won't sleep a wink over there, worrying about you. I told Herb I was coming. I even brought over my nightgown and my toothbrush. I can stay in Miss Rosie's room, since she's gone. And then you'll have company through the day when Danny goes to school. He does have to go to school, doesn't he?"

I could see that nobody was going to talk her out of it. I guess, with her there, I could just as well have gone home. Only now that I maybe had a choice, I didn't want to leave.

"Well," Miss Anna said uncertainly, "I guess Danny could sleep upstairs."

Mr. Holman grinned. I'd never seen him do that before. "If he's not afraid of that ghost up there, eh?"

"What ghost?" Miss Anna demanded sharply. "Don't be silly!"

"You believe in ghosts, boy?" Mr. Holman asked.

"No," I said and ladled some more gravy over my dumplings. "I don't believe in anything like that."

"Well, that's settled," Mrs. Holman said. "He's not afraid to sleep upstairs, and he can still burn the trash and carry in the wood. And I'll sleep in Miss Rosie's room and keep you company. Put my bag in there, Herb. That is your sister's room, isn't it? Off the dining room?"

So Mr. Holman went home, and his wife stayed, and Miss Anna dished her up some canned peaches for dessert with us. Mrs. Holman turned out to be the talkingest woman I ever heard. She acted as if I weren't there at all.

Well, I decided when I left the table, my chores had been pretty well laid out for me. Miss Anna kept some things to burn in the kitchen range, to start a fire with, but there were some other things she wanted me to take outside. I put some matches in my pocket and gathered up the boxes the grocery man had delivered groceries in and went out the back door.

Remembering what had happened to Miss Rosie, and the way I'd seen Mr. Holman in the backyard with a red can, I checked the trash barrel before I put a match into it.

And sure enough, I could smell gas.

What the heck was going on? Did he *want* someone to get hurt? I packed the cardboard into the barrel so it wouldn't blow away, but I didn't light it. I decided that tomorrow, on my way to take the contents of the jewelry box to the jeweler for appraisal, I'd stop and see what Ben Newton thought about a neighbor who'd pour gas into a person's trash barrel without telling them about it.

That was a long way off, though. First I had to get through the night.

I was feeling thoughtful when I went back into the house. I stood for a few minutes inside that long enclosed porch, thinking how anybody who had a key to the outside door could come in here and sneak up the back stairs if they wanted to, without ever being noticed by Miss Anna if she was alone. She didn't ever come out here, because there was a step down from the kitchen and she couldn't run her wheelchair over it. She was also hard of hearing, so if someone coming in or out didn't slam the door or stomp their feet, Miss Anna'd never know the difference.

Miss Rosie might hear them, of course. And she went in and out the back door. Would anyone dare come in this way when Miss Rosie was home? Or did they wait until she'd gone out to the store or something?

The thing was, the Holmans lived right next door. They could easily see when Miss Rosie left, and they probably knew about when she was likely to go out shopping or running her errands. They were supposed to be respectable people, but I guessed a lot of people were respectable right up to the time they decided to do something that wasn't very nice.

I didn't think it was nice of the Holmans to barge

in on us now, when Miss Anna had just told Mrs. Holman we didn't need her.

Sure enough, Mrs. Holman was taking over the best she could. She brought me a stack of sheets and a pillow and a quilt and a blanket. "Here. You can use these. Maybe you'd like to use one of the tower bedrooms. Boys always like towers."

She smiled, but I didn't smile back. If Miss Anna didn't say where I was to sleep, I'd pick my own place. As I remembered the towers, they all had peeling wallpaper and stains on the ceilings that suggested the roofs would leak if it rained.

There hadn't been any sign of a leak in the room that had once been Miss Rosie's, and it was right at the top of the stairs. It seemed as good a choice as any. I pulled the sheets off the furniture and made up the bed with the things Mrs. Holman had given me.

The room smelled odd, musty from being closed up and unheated for years, no doubt. I opened both windows. There was one that looked out toward the side yard and another one that opened onto the roof over the front porch, and the fresh air helped a lot.

Gramps had brought me some clothes, including pajamas (I bet Aunt Mattie packed the suitcase), and he'd included a flashlight I was glad to have. There was an overhead light with a twenty-five watt bulb in it; it made just enough illumination so I could see to find the bed after it got really dark.

It was still early, and I didn't want to go to sleep. But I didn't want to sit down in the parlor and listen to Mrs. Holman talk, either, so I stayed upstairs. Gramps had stuck a couple of my library books in with my school clothes, and I tried reading, but twenty-five watts aren't quite enough to read by. I could have used the flashlight, which was ten times brighter, only I was afraid I'd wear the batteries out and that I might need it, later on.

While I could still hear the voices floating up the stairway, and with the light on (feeble though it was), I didn't feel nervous. I stretched out on the bed with my hands behind my head and thought.

Mostly what I thought about was how insistent Mrs. Holman had been about spending the night in this house. Why? I wasn't fooled into thinking she was a kindly soul who just wanted to help a neighbor, because it was true Miss Anna didn't need her help.

No, Mrs. Holman, I decided, could be the one who had the key to the back door, but not to the other rooms in the house where she wanted to look. For the money, of course. And I didn't think she intended, if she found it, to hand it over to the Cat Ladies. I'd have bet anything she intended to take it home with her and never tell anyone where she got it. I wondered if she'd managed to sneak in sometimes and up the back stairs when the Cat Ladies were at the front of the house. Was it her face I'd seen in the upstairs windows?

The more I thought about it, the less I liked the idea that she could come and go up the back stairs and nobody would hear her. I wondered if there was any way to lock the door at the bottom of those stairs?

After a few minutes, I got up and went along the hall and down the stairs that led to the back porch. And sure enough, there was one of those sliding bolt things. I shoved the bolt over and knew nobody was going to use those stairs until the door was unlocked. Then I went back up to the front bedroom and stretched out on the bed again.

After a while, I heard Mrs. Holman calling "Good night, dear, and call me if you need anything! I'll sleep with my door open!" She said it very loudly, the way some people do with someone who's hard of hearing. I knew if you looked straight at Miss Anna and spoke in a normal tone, she usually knew what you'd said.

I supposed it was time to put out my own light, so I did; but I tucked the flashlight under my pillow where I could find it in a hurry if I needed it.

It was different with the lights out. There were creaking sounds, and I knew it was only the house adjusting to a different temperature, because Gramps' house made sounds, too. These were spookier, though.

I felt a long way from anybody, and I knew that if anything happened, Miss Anna couldn't do much about it, even if she heard it.

What did I think was likely to happen? It was true, what I'd said, that I didn't believe in ghosts. I'll have to admit, though, that the hairs stood up on the back of my neck when I heard the footsteps on the stairs. I sat up, straining to see through the blackness. I'd left my door open, resisting the urge to put a chair under the knob the way C.B. had suggested I do with the back door.

There was a streetlight outside, and the glow filtered through the leaves of the big oak in the front yard. Not much of it got inside the house.

The quilt was warm around me, but I felt cold. I reached under my pillow and closed my fingers around the flashlight.

Someone was climbing the stairs. Very slowly and carefully and quietly. Not the way someone would if they lived in the house, but the way a thief would. Sneaking.

It had to be Mrs. Holman, didn't it?

I knew it did, because the only other person in the house was Miss Anna. She couldn't walk more than a step or two, and she had to be holding onto something to do *that*.

I wasn't afraid of Mrs. Holman, was I? No, I decided. I wasn't. If I was sure it was really *her*.

The footsteps reached the top of the stairs and stopped. Right outside my doorway.

I held my breath and listened, and I could hear breathing.

It didn't sound like a woman's breathing.

Come to think of it, the footsteps hadn't sounded very light, either. I didn't remember that the stairs had creaked when I came up them, and Mrs. Holman didn't weigh much more than I did.

My scalp was prickling, and I had goose bumps all over.

What if it wasn't Mrs. Holman at all?

The breathing stopped, as if whoever it was had held his breath, too, to listen for *mine*.

I couldn't stand it any longer. I was scared, but I figured I'd be less scared if I knew who it was.

I pulled the flashlight out from under the covers and aimed it toward the doorway and flicked the switch.

12

The strong white light cut through the darkness and outlined a face and fuzzy head of hair.

Mr. Holman yelped and stepped backward, then stopped.

"Turn off that blasted light," he said. "Or at least point it somewhere besides in my eyes."

He was carrying a flashlight, too. If he had any legitimate business up here on the second floor—or even in the house—I thought he'd have his turned on, instead of sneaking around in the dark.

I dropped the beam of the flashlight so it wasn't in his face, but I didn't turn it off. "What do you want?" I demanded. I wasn't so scared any more, now that I knew who it was. I was more angry.

"I just came up to check, see if you were all right," he said.

If he expected me to believe that, he was stupider than he thought *I* was.

"I'm fine," I said. "Or I would be, if people would quit moving around so I could sleep."

"Yeah. Well, OK. Fine. Good night."

I didn't answer him, and after a few seconds, he turned and went back down the stairs, walking in a normal way. The stairs creaked under his weight, and he'd turned the light on so he could find his way.

He'd been checking on me, all right, hoping I was asleep so he could go do whatever he intended to do. And that was the reason his wife had insisted on staying in the house, so she could let *him* in after Miss Anna had gone to sleep.

On impulse, I jumped out of bed and ran, barefooted, to the stairs. I heard his wife murmur something, and all of a sudden curiosity overcame any nervousness I might have felt. I crept down to the landing—carefully, so the stairs didn't creak at all—and I stayed there in the shadows and heard what they said.

"That darned kid's still awake," Mr. Holman said. He wasn't speaking loudly, but I heard him, all right. "We'll have to wait. I'll come back in a couple of hours. He'll be asleep by then."

Mrs. Holman sounded nervous. "Maybe we ought to forget it, Herb. I talked to that old lady tonight before she went to bed, and she insists they've already found all the money her father hid."

He made an exasperated sound. "Listen. I've been working in that bank for thirty years, and I've seen all their deposits. They never put more than their Social Security checks in their account. Old man Caspitorian hid thousands of dollars, everybody knows he did. If they found it, what did they do with it? They didn't put it in the bank, and they didn't spend it on their house or themselves, so what did they do with it?"

His wife didn't answer, so he answered himself.

"They haven't found it, that's what. Maybe a few dollars here and there, that they spent in cash for living expenses. But there has to be a fortune still hidden somewhere in this house, and I'm going to find it if I have to take the place apart board by board!"

"What if that boy doesn't go to sleep now? Maybe you scared him so he'll stay awake. Maybe you'll have to come back tomorrow night."

"And what if you're not still here tomorrow night? What if he stays awake tomorrow night, too, and finds me here? Am I supposed to tell him I've got a key to the back door? If you'd come over here sooner, before she asked that kid to stay with her, we wouldn't have this problem."

"How was I supposed to know when to come over? I came as soon as I heard Rosie'd gone to the hospital," Mrs. Holman said.

They started moving away, and suddenly a cat

squawled an ear-splitting shriek and I nearly fell down the stairs.

I guess I wasn't any more scared than they were. Mr. Holman swore—real swear words, not like the ones Gramps uses—and then he remembered that Miss Anna was sleep only a few rooms away.

"Blasted cats. They're supposed to be able to see in the dark. Why don't they get out of the way? Listen, you'd better check on the old lady, see if that racket woke her up."

"No, no. Nothing will wake her up once she takes off that hearing aid for the night. She's deaf; how do you think I've gotten away with prowling around up over her head even when she's awake?"

Mr. Holman sure was a sourpuss. "Fat lot of good it's done," he said. "You haven't found anything but a few hundred-dollar bills for all the effort."

Mrs. Holman sounded as cross as her husband. "Well, if you think it's so easy, why don't *you* stay home and watch to see when Rosie goes out? Why don't *you* take a chance on being trapped up there when she comes home quicker than you expect? The last time I thought I'd never get a chance to sneak out, and what am I supposed to say if she catches me inside her house? 'Excuse me, I just happened to be searching your attic'? It's all right if I run the risks while you do the complaining, is that it?"

"Oh, for pete's sake," Mr. Holman said. "I'm going home. I'll be back after that kid's asleep."

They went off toward the kitchen, then, and I stood there shivering on the stairs, wondering what I ought to do.

I didn't think it would help to wake Miss Anna and tell her. I wasn't sure she'd believe me, and Mrs. Holman was such a talker she'd make *me* sound like the intruder, probably.

I wished there was a telephone so I could call Ben Newton. Or Gramps, even. Gramps would know what to do.

Or would he? What could I prove, if the Holmans said I was a liar? I couldn't prove that they had a key to the back door. I couldn't prove they'd found some money in the Caspitorian house and kept it for themselves. I couldn't prove Mr. Holman had been in here prowling around. All his wife had to say was that she'd been nervous and asked him to check through the house. Probably most grown-ups would believe that.

I couldn't even prove Mr. Holman had poured gasoline in the trash barrel, although I was certain he had.

Sometimes it's a pain, being an eleven-year-old kid.

I heard Mrs. Holman coming back, so I went upstairs and crawled into bed. It was quite a while before I stopped shivering. I didn't feel the least bit sleepy. How could I, when I kept expecting that Mr.

Holman would try to get past my door as soon as I dozed off?

Pretty soon I got an idea. How would it be if I built a barricade across the top of the stairs? That way, unless he used the flashlight, I'd know when Mr. Holman tried to come up there again.

It wasn't hard to find something to put across the stairs. There was enough junk in the rooms on the second floor to have built a barricade all the way across Main Street.

I used lightweight stuff that was easy to move. Chairs, mostly, and a couple of little night stand things. Good, I thought. That'll slow him down. I wonder what excuse he'll have for coming up again?

I got back into bed, and I was tired. I was sure I'd be able to go to sleep now, at least until Mr. Holman tried to sneak upstairs again. And I almost did. I was warm and comfortable and sleepy. And then I heard another noise.

I sat up, wishing my heart wasn't making such a pounding that I couldn't hear very well. What was it?

After a minute or two, I decided the noise wasn't inside the house, it was outside.

Somehow, that didn't make me any less apprehensive. Because it sounded like somebody was trying to get in.

Not Mr. Holman, I thought. He had a key, and besides, his wife would let him in.

Who, then?

And then there was a sound I recognized. A soft whine, the kind Leroy made when he wanted in or out of my bedroom at night.

Leroy?

I sprang out of bed and ran to the front window. "Leroy?" I kept it low, but he heard me. He barked once, and I shushed him. "Be still, you fool dog! How did you get loose? How did you find me?"

For once, I was glad he'd gotten loose, though. A houseful of cats was no place for a dog, I supposed. None of them were up there with me, though. In the morning I'd have to figure out what to do with him. But for right then, I was only too happy to have him for company.

I didn't bother to get dressed. I didn't expect to see anybody except Leroy. I leaned as far out the window as I could and said, "Stay. You hear me, Leroy? Stay right where you are. I'm coming down."

I almost forgot the barricade I'd set up. If I hadn't turned on the flashlight, I'd probably have waded into it myself.

As it was, I had to decide whether to take it apart so I could get through it, risk knocking it over if I tried to climb over, or go down the back stairs.

I finally decided it would be easier to use the other stairs. They were steep and the walls were so close on each side I wondered how the servants had ever gone up and down them carrying trays or water jugs, or whatever they did.

The door at the bottom opened onto the enclosed porch, at the opposite end from the rack that held the firewood. At least back there I didn't think Mrs. Holman would hear me, even if she were still awake, which I suspected she was. I switched off the flashlight and slid back the bolt, listening to make sure there wasn't anyone out there before I eased open the door.

Gradually my eyes adjusted to the light enough so I could see to walk toward the outer door. I was almost there when something brushed across my foot.

Rat! I thought, and almost yelled. And then it happened again, and I heard a tiny meow and realized how silly my first thought had been. There weren't any rats in this house, at least not in the part where the cats were. I reached down to touch the furry thing and guessed that it was Roscoe, the kitten we'd rescued.

"I think you'd be better off in the kitchen before I let Leroy in," I said. "Any more of your friends out here?"

I carefully opened the door into the kitchen and put Roscoe inside, hoping he was the only one accidentally left out here for the night. Then I crossed to the outer door and stuck my head out and whistled.

I heard him coming like a herd of elephants, and

before I could get out of the way Leroy crashed into me, nearly knocking me down. He was so tickled to see me, he licked my face and ears until I pulled him down.

"OK, OK! Calm down! I'm glad to see you, too! Come on in, and be quiet, understand? I don't want anyone to know you're here."

His toenails scratched on the floor, but he didn't make any more noise. He went with me, after I re-locked the door, up the back stairs and along the up-per hall; and when we reached my room, he climbed up on the bed just as if we were home.

It was funny what a difference it made, having Le-roy there with me. Before I knew it, I was asleep.

I woke up thinking the house was falling down around my ears and hearing someone screaming. I guess by then my hair was getting used to standing straight up on my head, because I hardly noticed it.

I figured it all out later; what had happened, I mean. By the time I told C.B. about it the next day, I could even laugh, though I didn't do any laughing at the time.

The way I figured it was that one of the cats, prob-ably Killer, had come upstairs. Mostly the cats stayed out of the second story, although Polly had gone with C.B. and me to the attic.

Anyway, Killer came upstairs, snooping the way

cats do. And Leroy woke up and found a strange cat in the room and did what dogs usually do to strange cats.

He chased it.

The trouble was, Leroy was in such a hurry and so excited he didn't notice my barricade. He hit it full bore after Killer had leaped over it. All those chairs and little tables falling down the stairs were what sounded as if the roof was caving in.

The noise must have been as frightening to him as it was to everybody else. And in his panic, he missed the turn in the stairs and crashed into the wall, where he got tangled up in the curtains from the window there on the landing. The curtains came down and covered his head, and Leroy kept right on going down the stairs.

Mrs. Holman was up and around, because she was fully dressed. I think she'd been about to check on me again, because she was right at the bottom of the stairs when this white-draped creature weighing almost as much as she did came hurtling toward her.

Leroy hit her solidly and knocked her flat. The cats, sleeping all over the place, woke up howling and spitting as Killer passed through with Leroy in hot pursuit. It didn't seem to slow Leroy down that he couldn't see where he was going; and about the time I got to the landing behind him, I heard another crash, and Mrs. Holman screamed again.

Even Miss Anna couldn't sleep through *that*. I heard her voice calling from her room beyond the dining room. "Who's that? What's going on?"

I wouldn't have had time to answer her, even if I'd known what was happening. I hadn't figured it out yet, though I did a minute later when I got the flashlight turned on the scene below.

Mrs. Holman was sprawled amidst broken china from a vase that had fallen off the tall wardrobe closet at the side of the hall. On top of the wardrobe Killer squatted, eyes shooting sparks when my light touched them, spitting angrily.

And Leroy, still with those torn curtains around his head, was bungling around the entrance hall trying to free himself, while cats scattered in every direction.

Mrs. Holman scrambled to her knees, and then to her feet, gasping for enough breath for another scream. Leroy ran toward her, and when they were practically nose to nose (only his was under the curtains), she made a noise as if she were being strangled, then turned and fled for the back of the house. I heard the door slam behind her when she left the porch.

"Here, boy! Here, sit! Sit, Leroy!"

I made a grab for him and managed to get the curtains off his head. Immediately he slowed down. I thought he might go berserk when he saw all those cats, though most of them were high enough above him to be safe by this time. Even little Roscoe had

sunk his baby claws into the curtains at the window beside the front door; he clung there, crying, until I lifted him down.

"What is it?" Miss Anna called. "Is the house afire?"

I hurried through the darkened rooms to her door, stubbing my toe on another flashlight. Mrs. Holman must have dropped it when Leroy hit her. "It's all right, Miss Anna. Just an accident. Something fell."

Boy, what an understatement that was!

"Oh. Nothing serious?" she asked.

"No. Just a broken vase. Killer—I mean, Chester —knocked it off the top of the wardrobe in the hall."

"Oh. All right. Don't cut yourself on the pieces."

"No. I'll clean it up," I said. "I'm sorry you got woke up."

"All right. Good night, Danny."

By the time I'd locked the door behind Mrs. Holman—and I did bring a chair from the kitchen to prop under the knob, although I suspected from the way she was shrieking when she left that she thought she'd been attacked by a ghost and she wouldn't be back for a while—there wasn't an awful lot left of the night.

What there was, though, I slept through. Leroy snuggled up against me and kept me company.

Nothing else happened until my alarm went off.

13

Being only a few blocks from school, I managed to get there early the next day. I'd had to explain to Miss Anna that Leroy had followed me, smelled me out somehow. I couldn't take him home, but she said it was OK if I chained him to a tree in the back yard. Luckily she had a chain from when they'd had a dog, twenty years ago. I guess they never disposed of anything they ever had, even a chain for a dog that had been dead for all that time.

I went the long way around so I could call home from the pay phone on the gas station lot. I figured I'd better tell Gramps where Leroy was so he wouldn't waste time looking for him. Aunt Mattie answered the phone, so I said Leroy was with me and not to worry. But I didn't say any more. I knew I'd never get to school at all if I started telling her what had happened during the night, and she might not even let me stay there the rest of the week.

I went across the school grounds and met Paul and Steve and Tubby and Frankie. For once they were talking about something besides baseball. Paul called out to me, so I joined them.

"Hey, Danny! You heard the latest?"

"No, what?" As long as it didn't involve me, I didn't care how horrible it was, whatever had happened, I thought.

"Tubby was going past the old Caspitorian house last night, and he saw lights in the upstairs! And then this morning his grandmother was talking to her next door neighbor, who lives across the street from the Cat Ladies, and she said Mrs. Holman saw a ghost there last night! A real ghost, trailing white robes and everything!"

For a minute I felt sort of stunned, and then I had to laugh. In fact, I laughed so hard I couldn't talk.

"What's so funny? We're not putting you on. It really happened! Tubby was riding home from his grandmother's with his folks, and they all saw the light! And Mrs. Holman—"

I struggled to stop laughing. "Mrs. Holman saw Leroy wrapped in a curtain that came down on him when he got tangled up in it chasing a cat. And the light was mine; I slept there last night because Miss Rosie had to go to the hospital, and Miss Anna didn't want to be all alone."

I expected they'd all laugh, too. Nobody did. In fact, the way they were looking at me, I didn't think they believed me.

"You're *staying* there?" Frankie asked. "In the *Caspitorian* house? And they let you bring that moose of a dog into the house with all their cats?"

"Well, they didn't exactly let me bring Leroy. He came on his own." I had to explain it, and I could see they were beginning to believe it was true. Frankie didn't appear to like it very much.

Maybe he realized that if I was staying in the house, I might capture old Killer. Up to then, I'm sure he thought I didn't have any chance at all.

"You making friends with Killer?" Steve asked. There was a note of respect in his voice.

"Well, he isn't exactly eating out of my hand yet," I said truthfully. "I'm just in the same house."

"You going to stay there again tonight?" Tubby asked. He must have eaten breakfast not more than an hour earlier, and already he was eating a banana, his cheeks filled like a squirrel's with two acorns in his mouth.

"Every night until Miss Rosie comes home, I guess," I said. I knew he was disappointed that it hadn't been a ghost in the house. "It's kind of a spooky old place. I haven't seen any real ghosts there yet, though."

173

All of a sudden Paul started to laugh. "I'll bet Mrs. Holman looked funny when she thought a ghost was coming at her! Did you see the whole thing, Danny?"

And then we were all laughing, and Paul slapped his leg the way Gramps sometimes does when he's amused. Only Frankie didn't laugh. He looked at me as if he'd like to step on me and squash me the way you'd squash a bug.

By noon the story was all over the school. Everybody like the idea of being scared by a ghost in a haunted house. But the idea of Leroy running around blinded by a curtain so that he'd frightened a neighbor woman half to death was so funny that they seemed happy to have that version of it to talk about.

"I wish I'd been there," C.B. said when I told her. "I'll bet it was hilarious."

I grinned. "To tell the truth, it's a lot funnier now than it was when it was happening. I don't know what Mrs. Holman told her husband, but they didn't come back. It makes me mad, though, to think they found some of the money Mr. Caspitorian hid, and they kept it."

"That's stealing, isn't it? And he's supposed to be honest enough to be a banker! I'm glad he doesn't work at our little Indian Lake bank. He's over at the Stockford branch. I'll bet they'd fire him if they knew. I wonder why the Caspitorian sisters don't bank here instead of twenty miles away?"

"There hasn't been a bank here for very many years, has there? Probably they'd always used the Stockford bank and never got around to changing when Tubby's dad opened this branch. Hey, you want to go with me to take the jewelry to Mr. Pritchard's?"

She did, so after school we went back to the old red house and got the box. I thought maybe Mrs. Holman might have come back during the day. She hadn't. I hoped she'd been scared enough to stay away permanently, though I doubted it.

We took the note from Miss Anna to the jewelry store, and I looked to see if Ben Newton was in his office. He wasn't, and the police cruiser was missing.

Mr. Pritchard read the note and then looked at the rings and things from the lacquered box.

"Is it worth anything?" I asked anxiously. He was looking at one of the rings through that little thing jewelers put over their eye so they can see better.

He didn't answer until he'd put down that piece and picked up one of the brooches. Then he sighed.

"It's worth something, certainly. Not what they hope, though, I'm afraid. I'll have to examine it more carefully before I can give them an offer, but off the top of my head I'd guess the entire collection isn't worth more than five or six hundred dollars. The few good stones would have to be reset, you see. I don't think I could sell any of the pieces the way they are."

Five or six hundred dollars. We both knew that wasn't enough to put a new roof on their house.

"Funny," C.B. said, kicking at the leaves that had fallen across the sidewalk as we walked away. "We haven't known them very long, but I feel as if they're friends, Miss Rosie and Miss Anna. Don't you?"

"They're nice," I agreed. I guess we were both depressed, after all the work we'd put in to find that jewel box, to learn that its contents weren't worth enough to help them out much.

We parted company at the end of Main Street. C.B. went home, and I went back to the Cat Ladies' house. I found Miss Anna basting a roast, and the smell was enough to make my mouth water.

"Your dog's been barking the last few minutes," she said, closing the oven door, her face all pink from the heat. Her hair was mussed, and for the first time I could see her hearing aid; I hadn't known she wore one until last night. "Maybe you'd better see if something is the matter."

So I went out into the back yard, and he had something to bark at, all right. Mrs. Holman was standing there, sort of cornered between the fence and the shed, looking both angry and frightened.

"Is this your dog? Get him away from me," she said. "He won't let me near the house."

"I don't think he'll bite. At least he never has," I told her. And then, because I didn't want her to think he wasn't any good as a watch dog, I added, "Unless someone tries to get in where they don't belong, of course. He doesn't like burglars."

She glared at me the way Miss Twitten had when the bag of liver broke and soaked my shirt with blood. "Well, I'm not a burglar. I just want to get my things from the house."

I walked over and made Leroy sit, standing with my hand on his head. "Go ahead. He won't hurt you. Not with me right here."

She took several steps and paused. "Is he going to be staying here with you?"

I didn't know if he was or not; I hadn't discussed it with Miss Anna. "Yes," I said. "He's a good watch dog. I feel better when he's with me; he sleeps at the foot of my bed."

Her face had been red; now it went sort of pale. I wondered if she knew it had been Leroy in a curtain that had scared her so last night. She didn't say anything more, only turned and went into the house. I hoped she was going to take her overnight bag home and not come back. I'd told her as plainly as I dared that as long as Leroy and I were there, she and her husband wouldn't get to do any more searching for old man Caspitorian's money.

I didn't go into the house until she was gone, carrying the little case with her night things. She didn't look at me, just went out the back gate and next door

177

to her own house.

I wasn't anxious to go inside because it meant telling Miss Anna what Mr. Pritchard had said about the jewelry.

She didn't seem upset, though. Just nodded. "I thought as much. Well, we aren't ready to be sent to the poorhouse yet. Maybe the roof will last another winter. I made some chocolate pudding for supper. Do you like chocolate pudding?"

I could see that she was trying to be nice to me. She wasn't bad-tempered, she only looked grim sometimes because of her arthritis. I thought maybe I'd look grim, too, if I hurt most of the time.

When Miss Anna wasn't looking, I saved a piece of the roast for Killer, and another bit for Polly. I knew I couldn't give some to each of the cats, but I had to do something to make Killer trust me.

When I went to feed the cats, though, Killer wasn't there. Polly took the meat and ate it quickly and daintily, before one of the other cats could snatch it, then rubbed appreciatively against my leg.

"K—I mean, Chester isn't here," I said. "Does he miss meals very often?"

"Oh, sometimes," Miss Anna said over her shoulder from where she was washing dishes. "They all go in and out as they please, and Chester roams more than any of the others. He'll show up in due time."

There was a cat door in the front of the house, one

of those swinging doors that a cat could push open from either side, big enough for Killer but too small for most dogs to follow through. It saved a lot of running for the sisters, Miss Anna said, because there was always a cat wanting in or out.

All through the evening, while I did my homework and Miss Anna sat reading, I kept waiting for Killer to come back. It wasn't until the following evening, though, when he *still* hadn't showed up, that I began to be afraid something had happened to him.

I didn't think the Holmans would come back until I'd left, but I didn't take any chances. I wedged the door shut again, so even if they used their stolen key, they couldn't get in. I'd introduced Leroy, very carefully, to some of the kittens, including Roscoe. He sniffed around them without frightening them at all, so then I took Polly out on the porch so she could meet him, too. I held her and talked to them both, telling Leroy to sit and be a gentleman.

He was eager to touch noses with her. Polly wasn't so eager. She allowed me to hold her close to Leroy though, very carefully, until I was certain he wasn't going to do anything stupid. Then I put her down and allowed them to sniff around each other. Leroy sat there with his tongue hanging out, looking at me as if to say that his behavior could be admirable when he wanted it to be.

I wished he could be trusted around all the cats so I could let him run free in the house the way he did at home. But I knew better. So I took him upstairs the back way, even though by this time I'd picked up what was left of my barricade and put the furniture back into an empty room.

Nothing disturbed my sleep that night. Nothing but the dreams I had about Killer, that he was gone and would never come back.

14

That was on Monday, and on Thursday Killer was still gone. At first Miss Anna wasn't really worried. After four days, though, she was quite concerned.

"He's never stayed away so long before. I hope nothing's happened to him," she said. "He does wander around. Maybe you could ask the neighbors if anyone's seen him."

So I walked around, up and down the street and on the next few streets over. Everybody in town knew Killer, but nobody had seen him for days, although several of them remembered seeing him walk the alley fence or stroll across a yard, they thought, maybe the previous Saturday or Sunday.

Nothing happened at the house, either. Miss Rosie had had her tests, and the doctor said she wasn't seriously ill, only needed rest. She could come home on

Saturday, he said.

So on Saturday I would go home. With or without having succeeded in catching Killer to win my way into the Secret Club.

I wasn't the only one who was thinking about that deadline. Paul and Steve, both looking troubled, told me that on Saturday they'd all be out at the place in the woods where they were going to be building the clubhouse.

"Do you think you can catch him?" Steve asked.

I shrugged. "I haven't given up yet," I said. "As a matter of fact, Killer's been gone for a couple of days. I haven't even seen him. So who knows?"

"He roams around a lot," Steve said. "I've seen him out by our place sometimes, and we're over a mile from where he lives. He'll probably turn up."

He didn't, though. On Friday morning Killer was still gone, and I met Frankie on the way to school. I didn't make any effort to catch up with him, but he saw me and waited.

"How you doing, capturing that old cat?" he greeted me.

"Still working on it," I said, not committing myself.

He laughed. I thought it was a nasty laugh. "Well, you have until six o'clock tomorrow to show up with him. Good luck!"

Somehow the gleam in his eye told me that he

didn't wish me any kind of luck except bad.

Steve and Paul must have mentioned to some of the other kids that Killer was missing. I didn't think anyone outside of the Secret Club members, and C.B., knew why I wanted him, but several kids I didn't even know came up to tell me where they'd seen Killer, and when.

Killer had a reputation in Indian Lake. None of the other cats or the dogs bothered him at all, and he came and went as he pleased. I found out he went all over town, and even the shut-ins, like Tubby's grandmother, knew what Killer looked like.

Strangely enough, nobody could remember seeing that cat after Sunday afternoon, *before* the last time I'd seen him myself.

It was almost as if he'd moved out of the house when I moved in, so I couldn't make friends with him. Or was it because of Leroy, who'd chased him down the stairs and probably scared him out of one or two of his nine lives?

I wasn't the only one who was concerned. Miss Anna was so upset she nibbled on her lower lip and her hand shook when she held her teacup.

"I know he wanders, but he's never stayed away so long before. He *always* comes back to eat," she said. "Some cats will go from door to door looking for handouts, but Chester never did. What he doesn't catch for himself, he eats at home, and he has a very good appetite. I hope nothing's happened to him. Maybe," she said, and she sounded on the edge of tears, "you'd try again to find him, Danny. I don't know what I'm going to tell Rosie when she comes home and he isn't here."

I looked around the big room with cats sitting on the windowsills, atop the wood box, and curled in the chairs. "Maybe there are enough other ones here so she won't miss him."

"Oh, she'll miss him," Miss Anna said. "If I could get around, I'd go out and scour the neighborhood, see if maybe he got locked into someone's garage or shed or something. If he heard me calling, he'd let me know."

"I'll look again," I told her. So I changed into my old jeans and shirt and took off, with Leroy trotting beside me.

I was walking back to the house after a couple of hours of seeing dozens of other people's cats when I heard a motor behind me. I turned as the sheriff's car rolled to a stop alongside of me.

Ben Newton stuck his head out the window. "Hello, there, boy. What mischief are you up to these days? How you making out with Miss Anna?"

"No mischief," I said, kicking at a rock on the edge of the road. "I'm looking for Killer—the one they call Chester—because Miss Anna's worried about him. We haven't seen him for almost a week."

Ben nodded. "I know the one, big black devil. I saw him stand off four dogs one day, finally sent them all ki-yiing in four different directions. He's a tough cat. He'll probably come home when he's ready."

When he was ready, if it was later than tomorrow, wasn't going to do me any good, though I didn't say that. What I did say was, "I need to talk to you, sir. I think I ought to report some things that are going on at the Caspitorian house."

Ben Newton grinned. "You see that ghost they're supposed to have?"

"I sort of created one of my own," I admitted, and then I told him all about Leroy draped in curtains and about the Holmans and the things I suspected.

Ben guffawed about Leroy, but he wasn't amused at all at the idea that the Holmans had a key to the house, nor about Miss Rosie's accidents, either.

"Why didn't you tell someone sooner, boy?" he asked.

"Well, the first thing was that fire blazing up in the trash barrel, and though she said she didn't put any gas in there, I thought maybe she really *had*," I said. "I mean, people do stupid things like using gas to start fires, even when they know better. And Miss Rosie's old. She might even have forgotten. Gramps says people sometimes get forgetful when they get older. Until I saw Mr. Holman with that red can, I didn't think someone else might have done it. Why would they want to make Miss Rosie get burned?"

Ben was thoughtful; his fingers beat a tattoo on the steering wheel. "Maybe to do just what was finally accomplished by loosening the boards so the firewood fell on her. I'll take a look and see if I can tell if someone *did* do that. It would only take a minor accident to put an old lady like Miss Rosie in the hospital. And probably they expected that if that happened, Miss Anna would have to go to a rest home, leaving the house empty so they could go in and look for that money."

"Miss Rosie says there isn't any money. That they've found it all. But Mr. Holman works at the bank where they have their account, and he says they've never put any *there*, nor spent any, either. So he thinks it's still there. And so does their nephew, I'm sure. He wants them out of the house, too."

Ben's fingers went motionless as he thought about it. "I know he does. Makes a regular pest of himself, wanting me to check on them, admit I think it isn't safe to leave them alone. I wonder if there's any chance Virgil Caspitorian and the Holmans are in cahoots? I mean, Virgil does visit once in a while, and it wouldn't be too hard to get hold of those keys if they were hanging in plain sight. Not take the whole ring, because that might be missed, but the door key, anyway. Hmmmm. You say the Holmans admitted they'd found some cash in the house and kept it?"

"One of the reasons I didn't talk to Gramps or you about it before was that I can't prove anything," I said. "I heard what they said to each other, but that's not proof, is it?"

"Nothing that will stand up in court," Ben said. "You let me think about it, Danny. We'll have to work out some way to trick them into giving themselves away."

"I'll only be there one more night," I said. "Tomorrow Miss Rosie comes home, and I'll leave then." If he set up a trap for the Holmans, I thought it would be neat to be in on it.

"Let me think about it," Ben repeated. "And I'll keep an eye out for that Killer cat, too, and let you know if I see him. In the meantime, you and Leroy stay out of trouble, you hear?"

"Yes, sir," I said. Ben waved and drove off, and I called Leroy back from where he was racing around a field pretending he was on the trail of a rabbit. At least I figured he was pretending, because I didn't see any rabbit.

We went on back to the Caspitorian house and found C.B. waiting for us. She'd been home since she left school, because she was wearing jeans and tennis shoes instead of the skirt and blouse she'd had on earlier.

She got up from the porch steps when she saw us. "You haven't found Killer."

"No." I was tired. "Miss Anna's upset because he's gone, but I don't know what else to do to find him."

"I know she is. She had tears in her eyes when she told me about him. What are you going to do now, Danny?"

I shrugged. "I don't know." I guess I looked as discouraged as I felt, and Leroy nuzzled my hand as if he sympathized with me. "Miss Anna thinks he may be trapped in somebody's garage or something. I don't know how we'll find him if that's happened. And if it's someone who's gone away on a trip or something, who knows when he'll get out?"

C.B.'s face was grave. "How long could he live without food and water?"

I wasn't sure. I didn't think it would be more than a week or so. Even that wouldn't be very pleasant.

"Remember the time we were looking for Leroy," she said, "and he was locked in that shed? Maybe Killer will escape, too."

"If he's missing because he's locked in somewhere, he'd already have escaped by now, if he could," I said glumly.

"I guess you're right. Hey, what's the sheriff coming here for?"

I turned around and sure enough, there was the police car pulling up at the front gate. We both went out to meet it, Leroy tagging along.

Ben Newton stuck his head out of the window, the

same as he had to talk to me earlier. "Young lady, do you know your mother is looking for you?"

C.B. made a sound of disgust. "I *told* her I was going to see Danny."

"That was hours ago. She expected you back for supper. Come on, I'll give you a lift home. I have to go out that way anyhow."

C.B. went around and opened the car door and slid in beside him. "This is silly. Sending the police car after me because I'm late for supper!"

Ben chuckled. "Be glad that's all it's for. Say, there's our friend Mr. Holman coming home from work. I wonder . . . do you suppose he carries that key to Miss Rosie's back door with the rest of his keys?"

I felt a surge of excitement. "Would that prove something? If he does?"

"I think so. With that as evidence, your word about what you heard him say would carry more weight." Ben turned off the engine. "I think I'll speak to Mr. Holman."

The neighbor had driven into his yard right alongside of us, and he looked curiously in our direction when he got out of his car. He took a few steps toward us when he saw C.B. sitting in the police cruiser.

"Evening, Mr. Holman," the sheriff said pleasantly.

"Good evening, Sheriff." Mr. Holman came right up to the car, and Ben opened the door and got out.

"Some trouble with these kids, is there?"

"Always trouble with kids," Ben said. "Especially that one." He nodded in my direction. "Him and his dog, always into something."

Mr. Holman smiled in satisfaction. "I've noticed that. Always where he doesn't belong," he said.

Boy, I thought, he's a great one to talk. But I didn't say anything. Whatever Ben had in mind, I hoped it worked.

"Sometimes, though," Ben said, standing with one hand atop the open door of the police car, "kids notice things that are useful. That reminds me, Mr. Holman. You have your keys on you?"

"My keys?" For a few seconds he looked blank, and then Mr. Holman shot a suspicious glance in my direction. He had no reason to suspect that I knew he'd stolen a key to the Cat Ladies' back door, but the question made him uneasy. We could tell that. "Sure, I'm carrying my keys. Bank keys, car keys, house keys. Why?"

"I wonder if you'd let me look at them," Ben said. He was still talking in that easy way he had, not sounding dangerous at all.

"Look at them?" Mr. Holman echoed. I could see that he didn't like that idea, although he wasn't sure what this was all about. "Why on earth would you want to look at my keys?"

"Routine," the sheriff said. "Of course, you don't

have to let me look at them. I don't have a warrant or anything like that. Only if you have nothing to hide, it shouldn't be a big deal."

Mr. Holman was looking distinctly nervous now. "Of course I have nothing to hide! I don't understand. What are you getting at?"

"You said you have the keys to the bank where you work? You're sure you have them all? Haven't lost one?"

I thought there was a trace of relief in the man's eyes, although he was trying not to reveal anything. "Why, has something happened at the bank? I just left it half an hour ago . . ." Already he was fumbling for the ring of keys in his pants pocket, sorting through them. "Yes, see? Here's the one for the front door, and this one—"

"How about this one here?" Ben asked, reaching over and picking out a big, old-fashioned-looking key, larger than the others. "What's this one for?"

Even from where I stood, on the other side of the police car, I could see that *that* key had been marked. There was tape on it, and I knew there would be printing on the tape, that the key was marked as all the others were marked for the Caspitorian house.

Too late Mr. Holman realized he'd been tricked by the supposed interest in his bank keys. He shot me a look of pure hatred, although he was still trying to keep up the pretense of innocence.

"Why, I don't remember, offhand. What's this all about, sheriff? That isn't one of the bank keys, it's a personal one."

Ben nodded, reading the tiny letters on the tape. "Personal, yes. Says *Back Door*. Does it fit *your* back door, Mr. Holman?"

"Why . . ." I think he'd been about to say *yes*, that it did, and then he thought better of it. An outright lie that could, within two minutes, be proved to be a lie, might not be wise.

"Or does it fit somebody else's back door?" Ben Newton asked softly. "Does it, maybe, fit the *Caspitorians'* back door?"

"Oh, maybe it does." Mr. Holman was thinking fast. "Maybe so. Virgil gave me a key some time ago. Haven't had any occasion to use it, but he thought I ought to have one."

"Virgil Caspitorian gave it to you? Why would he do that, Mr. Holman?"

Ben's voice was so calm, so kind, so ordinary. I wondered if this was how he questioned criminals, so that before they realized what he was doing, he'd led them into trapping themselves.

I sure hoped he was going to trap Mr. Holman.

Mr. Holman had a rather strained expression. "Why ever would you want to know that, Sheriff? You can check with Virgil, if you like. He'll tell you he gave me the key."

"Well, it isn't *his* key or *his* house, and I don't think his aunts know you have it," Ben said, keeping his tone mild. "So it doesn't seem unreasonable to me to want to know why he gave it to you. Of course, I can call him up and ask him, but since we're standing here face-to-face, is there any reason why *you* can't tell me?"

Mr. Holman was stiff; even his lips moved stiffly. "I suppose not, although I think this is rather irregular. Virgil thought someone close by should have access to the house in case something happened to his aunts. Old ladies like that, they might fall and not be able to get help."

In that case, I thought angrily, all they'd have had to do was tell the old ladies themselves what they meant to do and not be so sly about it.

"Hmmmm," Ben murmured. "I see. Did Virgil Caspitorian also suggest that you arrange some accidents for his aunts, so that you'd have something to check on?"

That really hit hard. C.B. said afterward she could watch the color going out of Mr. Holman's face, as if the red line were dropping in a thermometer.

"I don't know what you mean, Sheriff," Mr. Holman said, but we all knew he was lying.

"I mean," Ben said, still mild-mannered, yet with one hand resting casually on the gun handle that protruded from his holster, "like pouring gas into their trash barrel so the flames would flare up when they tried to use it. Wait a minute, sir, don't deny it too soon," for Mr. Holman had opened his mouth to speak, "because we have witnesses who saw you with a gas can out there."

The man shot me a look that must have been like the one I had when I wanted to kick Leroy. His throat worked as he bit back the words he'd intended to say.

"Two witnesses," the sheriff said, not looking at either C.B. or me at all. "They were concerned about it, naturally. And then there's the matter of loosening that board that held their firewood in place. Actually, I think that could be construed as an assault against an old woman who is now in the hospital because of it. That's a serious charge, Mr. Holman. Very serious."

Mr. Holman made a curious sound, deep in his throat, and still didn't say anything.

"And there's the matter of the money you found in the Caspitorian house," Ben Newton went on. "Does Virgil know you found it and kept it? Were you supposed to be looking for it for him? Was it his idea to arrange for the accidents? Or did you think of those things yourself?"

Mr. Holman had been very pale. Now his face suddenly flushed with anger. "I don't know where you got all these crazy ideas! You can't prove a thing, Sheriff! You don't have any evidence against me!"

194

The keys jangled softly in Ben's hand as he jiggled them. "Only this key, sir. A key to the Caspitorian house, a key the old ladies don't know you have. It will add considerable weight to the testimony of the witnesses."

"Testimony?" Testimony meant going to court, being charged with a crime, didn't it? And Mr. Holman was a banker, a man who was supposed to be trustworthy with other people's money. What would his employers think about it, if he were charged with the things Ben Newton was talking about?

"Are you charging me with something, Sheriff?"

"Well, at this stage let's just say I'm investigating. Why don't you tell your wife you'll be a little bit late for supper, and you come on over to my office. I'll call Virgil Caspitorian and get him over there, too, and we'll talk about the situation. OK? You can follow me in just a few minutes; I have to run this little girl home, but I won't be more than fifteen minutes."

Nobody could have looked at Mr. Holman without realizing that he was badly shaken. Even if Virgil had given him the key, and I didn't doubt it because it would have been easier for Virgil to get it in the first place, Mr. Holman still knew that having it was wrong.

Anyway, I thought, as the police car drove off, there wouldn't be any more of those middle-of-the-night intrusions, or Mrs. Holman getting into the house to look for things when the old sisters didn't know about it. At least nobody would plan any more "accidents" for them.

Which was great, I supposed. It was one problem solved. Now all I had to do was find—and catch—Killer, before this time tomorrow night.

I didn't have much hope that I was going to be able to do it.

15

Saturday was a beautiful fall day, clear and sunny and just cool enough so it felt good to wear a sweater. I thought about the kids out in the woods building their Secret Club clubhouse and wondered if I'd ever get to be part of the group. Nobody at Indian Lake School had been unfriendly, exactly, but nobody other than Paul and Tubby and Steve (I didn't think I could count Frankie) had actually made friends with me, either.

I went downstairs and got out the cat food for all the dishes. Miss Anna rolled her chair into the kitchen and regarded me with a hopeless air. "I don't suppose Chester has come back yet?"

I shook my head, unable to speak. I'd suddenly had the sensation of my throat closing, so there was an ache in it. I wasn't sure if it was concern for Killer or for the Cat Ladies or for myself.

The rest of the cats came to eat. They all had healthy appetites. I guess Miss Anna didn't, any more than I did. She made French toast for us. We weren't very hungry, so Leroy got most of it.

I packed all my stuff together for Aunt Mattie to take home when she came to pick it up. I'd already decided I wasn't going home yet. I was going to walk all over town again, asking people if they'd seen Killer. And if there were any places I thought he could have been accidentally trapped, I'd check those out, too.

Miss Rosie came home about the time we were clearing away the breakfast things. The doctor came into the house with her and made sure she sat down right away, because he said she was a bit wobbly. In most places I don't think the doctors even make house calls any more, let alone take their patients to and from the hospital, but Indian Lake is still old-fashioned, Aunt Mattie says. People still believe in helping one another, even the doctors.

"You all right?" Miss Anna asked her sister, and Miss Rosie smiled.

"Certainly. I'm fine. My bruises haven't all faded yet, but I'm fine. Did you find Mama's jewelry box while I was gone?"

"Danny found it," Miss Anna said, because that ache was still in my throat and I didn't feel like talking, especially not about anything bad. "The jewelry isn't worth much, though. Not enough to cover the taxes."

"Oh. Well, I guess I didn't expect it would be. I guess we'll have to dip into our reserve, then." Miss Rosie sighed, though she was smiling. "My, it's good to be home."

I pricked up my ears at that. Did that mean they still had some of their father's money? But where was it? If it wasn't in the bank, then it must be hidden around the house. That was enough to give me cold chills, even if Ben Newton *had* taken Mr. Holman in for questioning. *Virgil* wasn't under arrest for anything.

I cleared my throat. I had to warn them. "I hope you haven't got any cash hidden in the house. Somebody might find it, somebody not honest enough to give it back to you."

Miss Rosie laughed. "Oh, I don't think they'll find it. Do you, Anna?"

Miss Anna didn't laugh, though. Her fingers were white-knuckled on the wheels of her chair. "He's gone, Rosie. Chester's been gone since last weekend. Danny's been looking for him, but he hasn't found him. Since last weekend."

I didn't see what Killer had to do with the money they had hidden. Maybe Miss Anna was so upset she couldn't talk about one thing when she was thinking about something else, and she'd been dreading telling her sister about that cat.

Miss Rosie sat very still, although her lips trembled enough so I could tell. "Gone? Maybe he'll come back."

"He's never stayed away so long before," Miss Anna said.

"But he *could* come back. Even after a week. Couldn't he?" she asked me.

I couldn't answer that. "I'll leave my suitcase near the front door for Aunt Mattie when she comes. But I'll go out and look for K—for Chester. I'll try to find him," I told them.

And all the while I was wondering if it was wrong to let them hope that way, when I really didn't expect to find him. I'd been all over town already, and nobody had seen him since I'd seen him myself. I remembered him, eyes in amber slits and hair standing on end all over his body, atop that wardrobe thing in the front hallway after Leroy had chased him down the stairs.

Was that it? Had Killer simply left home because Leroy was in the house? Was it *my* fault he'd gone away?

I hadn't thought of that before, and it made me feel sick. But if that was the case, at least it didn't mean he was dead; someone could have taken him in.

When I really thought about it, that didn't seem

likely, because he was a big, distinctive-looking cat, and I was pretty sure everybody in Indian Lake knew who he belonged to. Still, maybe if Leroy and I left, Killer would come home. I said so.

"Maybe he will," Miss Rosie said anxiously. "Maybe he will."

Aunt Mattie rang the doorbell right about then, and we had to go through all that mush of my being thanked and Aunt Mattie asking about how I'd behaved—as if I wasn't eleven years old and didn't know some basic manners!—and the Cat Ladies invited me to come back anytime.

It was a relief to get out of there. I found that C.B. had ridden in with Aunt Mattie, and she'd packed a lunch and was wearing her "hunting clothes," as she called them.

"To help you look for Killer," she said.

"It's nice to know I've got one friend in this town," I told her. "Besides Leroy, who's sometimes more trouble than an enemy would be."

Leroy, hearing his name, wagged his tail and licked at my elbow.

"It's too bad Leroy can't track Killer, the way he did those bank robbers," C.B. said. "Can't you tell where he went, Leroy? Couldn't you smell him out, the way you do with Danny?"

"Maybe he could if we had something that smelled like Killer to start with. He had one of the bank robber's neckerchiefs, remember? And I guess he knows what *I* smell like. Besides that, he knows the places I go, so he has a clue about where to look. We don't have any clues about where Killer's gone. He wanders all over town."

"I wonder if he wanders out of town? Into the country, maybe? I'll bet he catches mice and things, and they'd be more plentiful in the country, wouldn't they? Like around old barns and sheds and in the fields?"

"I went into the country a little ways on that side of town." I waved an arm. "OK, let's try the other side. What have we got to lose?"

It was just coincidence that the direction we picked was the same direction as the Secret Club members were going to work on their clubhouse. I didn't intend to go out there and see what they were doing until I was eligible to be a member, too.

Anyway, we met the whole bunch of them. I'd seen the other guys, though I didn't know them all by name. They had lunch sacks, too, and most of them carried assorted tools: a saw, some hammers, that kind of stuff.

"You giving up on your initiation?" Frankie greeted me, grinning.

I saw C.B. stiffen. She didn't say anything, but her face looked like Mr. Holman's when the sheriff was questioning him.

"When I do give up, I'll let you know," I told him. I tried not to sound hostile, and I wasn't sure I succeeded.

"You know we wish you luck, Danny," Paul said.

"Sure. Thanks."

"Yeah," Tubby said, peeling a candy bar. "We hope you make it, Danny. We want you in the club."

"You got until six o'clock tonight," Frankie said, the grin still splitting his face. "We're gonna be out at the clubhouse until then. Paul told you where it is, right? We brought hot dogs and buns, and we're gonna have our supper out there. If you bring Killer in time, you can eat with us."

He said it so cheerfully that I knew he didn't expect me to be there. He glanced at C.B. and added, as if she couldn't hear him, "Too bad you have to play with girls if you don't make it into the club. But I guess that's what you're used to, playing with girls."

"I like some girls a lot more than some guys I've met," I said. I was feeling an uncomfortable shaking sensation in the pit of my stomach, though. I liked C.B. all right—in fact, I liked her a lot—but I didn't want to have to tell my dad I hadn't done anything with the boys the whole time I was in Indian Lake, that I didn't have any friends except a girl who was a newcomer like me.

"Well, see you around, Danny," Frankie said, and there was something in his eyes as he waved us good-bye that made me think he was sure I wasn't ever going to get into his club.

We stood there in the road until they disappeared around the corner, heading for the woods along the lake.

"I don't know why Frankie dislikes me so much," I said finally. "I never did anything to him that I know of."

C.B. scooped up a rock and threw it violently against a telephone pole to show how *she* felt.

"He's a stinker. You know what, I'll bet he's afraid of you, Danny. That's why he's so nasty to you, why he gave you such a rotten initiation stunt to do."

"Afraid of me?" I was astonished. "He's bigger and older than I am, and he's the leader of the Secret Club and a better ballplayer than I'll be if I practice until I'm as old as Gramps! Why should Frankie be afraid of me?"

"I don't mean afraid you'll beat him up, though that might not be a bad idea. No, I mean he's afraid you'll take over. As a leader. Maybe as the leader of the Secret Club, maybe win the kids away from following him. Because they *like* you, Danny. I can tell it, with everybody except Frankie. They admire you. You helped rescue Mrs. Trentwood's dog, and you found the money the robbers took from the bank, and you and Leroy saved my little nephew from drowning. You got your picture in the paper, and everybody knows how you helped capture the kidnappers. Frankie can't . . ." She groped for the right word. ". . . he can't *compete* with you. Besides that, you're smart in school, and he isn't. That's why he's afraid of you. He doesn't want you to be the leader instead of him."

"Huh." I wondered if she was right. "Well, I don't especially want to be the leader, or take Frankie's place in anything. But I don't want him to think he can push me around. He's convinced I'm going to fall on my face, though, that I'm not going to come through with Killer by tonight. No reason why he shouldn't be sure, I guess. *I* don't think I'm going to do it, either."

"Don't give up yet. It's only eleven o'clock. We have all day. Listen, Danny, let's go back that way instead of the way they went. I don't want to talk to them again until after you have Killer."

She indicated the road some of the kids had come down, one that curved out around the edge of town.

"OK. I don't want to see them again, either. You know, it's not just for me that I'm looking for Killer now. Miss Rosie and Miss Anna are really upset that he's gone."

And then I remembered the things they'd said that morning, and I repeated them to C.B. "It was funny, the way Miss Rosie said they'd have to dip into their reserve, after all, and Miss Anna didn't answer that. She said that Killer was gone, as if there was some connection."

C.B. shook her head. "I don't know. Shall we stop at each house and ask if they've seen a big, mean, black cat wearing a collar with diamonds set in it?"

"Diamonds?" I started to laugh, and then I choked on it, while C.B. was saying, "Well, they *look* like diamonds."

"Hey! Hey, wait!" I said and stopped in the middle of the dusty road, excitement beginning to run through me so that I prickled all over. "What if they *are* diamonds? Really? What if it's not only Killer they're upset about, but his collar!"

One of the things I liked about C.B. was the way she never acted as if I were crazy when I said something wild. She stared at me, her green eyes getting bigger and bigger. "You mean their father's money was spent for diamonds, and they put them into their cats' collars?"

I thought of all those jeweled collars, thirty-two or thirty-three of them.

"I don't know. Seems like even a fortune wouldn't pay for that many diamonds. I know they got the collars wholesale, so they weren't terribly expensive. But what if they put diamonds into some of them? What if old Mr. Caspitorian hid diamonds in the first place, instead of money? He might have! He was a jeweler, he could have had a lot of his fortune in diamonds when he got sick, and it was those he hid, and that's what they found! And Miss Anna used to work with her father, remember? She has the tools, she could have put them in the collars herself. Maybe into Killer's, because he's big and tough and they didn't think it was likely anything would happen to him, the way it might to a kitten like Roscoe."

Her mouth was open. "That would be an awfully foolish thing to do," she said slowly. "I mean, the money would have been a lot safer in a bank."

"Sure. Only maybe, like their father, they didn't trust the bank with a lot of money. In the depression when they were young, the banks all failed and people lost the money they had in them. I heard Gramps talking about it. And we know they don't trust Virgil. Maybe they thought if they had the money in the usual places, he'd manage to get his hands on it."

The more I thought about it, the more possible it seemed. "In fact, I'll bet that's one reason they didn't want it in the bank. Because if Virgil knew how much there was, and where it was, he'd figure out some way to get it. Remember how he came out to our house and tried to talk Gramps and Aunt Mattie into saying his aunts were senile and should be put in a rest home? If he got a court order to do that, maybe he could have gotten a court order to control their money, too."

"But to put something as valuable as diamonds into a cat's collar . . ." She didn't know whether to think I was crazy or not. "Golly, Danny, if you're right, what if the only collar that's important is Killer's? What if the others have just glass? So that if Killer's collar is missing, they don't have anything?"

"Then we have to find him," I said. And for the first time I thought maybe we *could* find him, because it was important. Not just to me, but to those nice old ladies.

We started along the road, and at every house we stopped and explained to whoever was there that we were looking for a big black cat with a red collar with jewels in it.

Nobody had seen Killer. Until we came to a tiny little house with an enormous garden where a man was out looking at his squashes and pumpkins. He stroked his chin and thought about it.

"Can't remember when it was. Week or more ago I saw a cat might have been like that. I think it was dead, though."

"Dead?" Sick, we didn't dare to look at each other. "Hit by a car, you mean?"

"I don't know about that, but it looked dead. A kid was carrying it in a little cage, one of those like you transport rabbits in, wire mesh, you know? And it just laid there like it was dead. I figured he was taking it home to bury it."

The sickness deepened. "And it was a big black cat, with white feet?"

"That's right." The old man nodded.

"Who . . . who was the kid carrying him?"

"Dunno," the old man said. "So many kids live on down this road. Can't tell 'em apart. They all wear the same clothes, just alike. Blue jeans and T-shirts and tennis shoes, just like you kids."

C.B.'s tongue snaked over her lips. "How old was he, then? Could you remember that? A big kid? A little one?"

He scratched his head, as if that would help him to think better. "Well, I wasn't paying all that much attention, you know. He wasn't a high school boy, I don't think. But maybe bigger than you are. Wasn't it his own cat?"

"Not if it was Killer," I said, and the ache was back in my throat.

"Funny. Why would he bury the cat if it wasn't his?" the old man said. "Say, you kids want a pumpkin for Halloween?"

I couldn't answer. After a moment, C.B. said, "No, thank you. Not today."

"No, no, not today. It's too early. But when it's time, you come out and get it from me. I'll let you pick out whichever one you want," he said.

We thanked him and went back out onto the road, neither of us saying anything for a few minutes. We stopped, then, and looked on down the road ahead of us.

"Is there any use in going on looking, if he's dead?" I said.

"We don't *know* that he's dead," C.B. pointed out. "It might not have been Killer, anyway. And besides, even if he's dead, we might find the collar."

I looked on down the gravel road. "Sure," I said. "It could have been a different cat. There are lots of black cats," but I didn't believe it. "I guess we'd better keep looking, though. Because even if Killer's . . ." The word stuck in my throat. ". . . even if he's dead, we ought to try to get his collar back. Just in case we're right about it."

We didn't talk much after that, except to speak to people at the houses. We asked the same questions we'd been asking, except that now we'd added another one: "Do you know a kid about my age who carried a cat in a cage, or maybe buried a cat?"

No one except the old man with the pumpkins had seen either a boy carrying a cat or a cat by itself. This was a dead end road, though. If a boy had gone past, his destination must have been somewhere on this road. So we kept on going, asking at all the houses on the right side, figuring we'd stop at the ones on the other side of the road on the way back.

It got to be lunchtime. We didn't feel like eating, so we kept on walking. And then, all of a sudden as we were passing a small farm, C.B. grabbed my arm.

"Danny! Look!"

I stared across a grassy field toward an old red brick house. There were chickens in the yard, cages of some kind against a small barn, and beyond the barn, there was a shed with a shingled roof with holes in it.

"What?" I asked. "Did you see something?"

"There! The name on the mailbox!"

I read the name, and I started to get tight and angry. So angry I thought I'd explode with it.

The name on the mailbox was Frank Sloan.

16

"Frankie!" C.B. said. "Did you know Frankie lived out here, Danny?"

"No." I stared at the red brick house. A curtain fluttered in an open window, but there was nobody around, no car in the yard. My gaze shifted to the cages, which took on new meaning. "Those are rabbit hutches, aren't they? The pumpkin man said the kid was carrying a cat in the kind of cage you'd use to transport rabbits."

"Frankie wouldn't have hurt Killer to make sure you didn't get into the Secret Club, would he? Nobody would be that mean, that rotten." She said it as if she didn't believe what she was saying, and I didn't, either.

"Frankie might have done anything. He doesn't want me in the club. He didn't want to come right out and say so, though. The other guys might have all voted against him."

"They might even have kicked him out as president," C.B. said. "Danny, maybe Killer isn't dead, maybe Frankie only captured him and shut him up until your deadline has passed—"

"How did he capture him? Why did the pumpkin man think he was dead?" I asked fiercely. "Nobody —I mean, nobody—could walk up and stuff that cat into a cage. Come on, let's see if anyone's home."

"What are we going to say if they are?"

"We're going to tell them we're looking for a cat and ask to look around. Keep your eye out for— for a place that looks like it's been dug up."

We walked up the driveway, and I recognized Frankie's bike on the front porch. It was a practically new, red ten-speed that he rode to school every day.

No one answered the door when we knocked.

"What are we going to do now?" C.B. asked. She was looking at a flowerbed that had been recently spaded.

"Look around," I said.

"What if they come home and catch us?"

"If they get annoyed about it, I'll ask them to call the sheriff," I said, although my heart was beginning to pound. "Come on."

We went out by the rabbit hutches. There were about twenty rabbits, all of them white ones. There certainly wasn't a black cat in any of the cages. Leroy touched his nose curiously to the wire mesh, and the rabbits backed away from him, huddling in the far corners.

We could see right away that it would have been hard to lock an animal into the barn. It was open in too many places that a climbing cat could reach.

Except for that one flowerbed in front of the house, we didn't see any places that looked as if they could be graves. If he'd killed Killer, would Frankie have dared bury him in plain sight, though? Wouldn't his folks have wondered what he was doing and asked questions?

"There's still the shed," I said. "Let's try that."

We walked across the hard-packed earth of the yard and then onto the grass around the shed. It didn't look promising. It looked, in fact, as if nobody had been near it in years. There wasn't even a pathway to the door of it, and there was a rusty hasp holding the door shut, though there was no padlock in it.

"Killer?" I said. "I mean, Chester, do you hear me?"

There wasn't any sound except a chicken clucking somewhere behind us.

"Shall we look inside?" C.B. asked uncertainly.

I only hesitated for a second or two. "Sure. Let's find out," I said, although I was sure that if Killer were inside he'd make some sound when he heard voices.

I unhooked the door and pulled it slowly open, peering into the gloomy interior. There weren't any windows, and only a few holes in the roof where the shingles were missing that let in a few beams of light.

"If he was in here, he'd be rushing past us to get out," I said. I felt my eyes stinging. "Well, I don't know where else to look."

I stepped back and was about to close the door when Leroy came around the corner. He thrust his nose past me, then whined, and a moment later he was inside, making peculiar frantic-sounding cries.

"He's found something," C.B. said, just above a whisper.

I didn't see how it could be Killer, but I stepped inside, anyway, waiting until my eyes adjusted a bit to the dimness. Leroy was over against the far wall, leaping up and whining.

And then I saw him.

Killer.

He was dead, I thought. He was hanging on a nail on the wall, hanging by that red collar with the jewels in it. It was too dark for the jewels to pick up any sparkle, but I could see the darker mass of black fur in the shadows.

Hanging? Killer, hanging?

I lunged across the dirt floor, tripping over an empty cage I hadn't seen, scraping my shin and hardly feeling it.

I was saying swear words, my dad's swear words, and I think I was half-crying, too, although I didn't notice the moisture on my face until later.

I reached out to take him down from the nail, which had caught under his collar, choking him—and he made a sound. A faint, tiny sound. His eyes were closed, but Killer was alive!

C.B. was beside me, her hands reaching up with mine to lift him. And then we saw, when we were right beside him, why he hadn't choked to death with his collar caught on that nail. There was a brace between the studs on the wall, and his hind feet just reached it. Killer was standing on that stud, and it had kept him from dying.

He made no protest when I managed to loosen his collar and lift him down. My heart was pounding so noisily I couldn't hear if he made any sound now or not.

I could feel his bones through the softness of his fur.

We took him outside into the sunshine, and I saw that there were tears on C.B.'s cheeks, too.

"He must have been there all the time he's been missing," C.B. said, sounding choked. She wiped her nose on the back of her hand. "Hanging there for five or six days. With nothing to eat or drink and that collar strangling him."

"Where's the lunch? Let's see if he can eat anything," I said. I could hardly think about Killer, really. I was thinking about Frankie, about a boy who would do such a rotten thing, about what I'd like to do to him when I caught up with him again.

There was a tuna fish sandwich in the lunch sack, and C.B. tried to feed it to him, but Killer couldn't swallow it. He didn't even try.

"We've got to get him to the vet," I said. "Come on. Let's go."

We walked back to town a lot faster than we'd walked out. We would have run as much of it as we could if we hadn't been afraid it would hurt Killer more.

We walked so fast our legs were aching; and though she didn't say anything, I could tell by the way C.B. pressed her hand against her chest that that was hurting, too. Even after starving for a week, Killer was heavy enough so it felt as if my arms would fall off.

"I wish someone we know would come by and give us a ride," C.B. said once. "Only I guess we're on the wrong side of town for that."

"Do you know where the veterinarian's office is?" I asked as we came to the edge of town. "Steve's dad's place?"

C.B. nodded. "We had to take Marcella there for shots. It's behind the Catholic church. I don't know if he's there on Saturdays, though."

I hadn't thought about that. I gritted my teeth. "Then we'll call him at home and tell him it's an emergency."

Just then I looked down the street and saw a familiar vehicle coming toward us.

"Flag him down, C.B.! It's the sheriff! Wave your arms!"

He pulled to a stop, not smiling. "I can't spend all my time with you kids, you know. Once in a while I have serious police business."

I didn't bother to argue with him. "We need to get Killer to Dr. Baker," I told him. "He's nearly dead. That rotten Frankie had him locked up in a shed, and somehow he got hanged from a nail. If he hadn't been able to touch his back feet to a cross-piece, he'd have strangled. He hasn't even opened his eyes since we took him down."

Ben took one look at Killer and reached around to open the back door of the car.

"Get in," he said.

Dr. Baker met us at the clinic after Ben called in on his radio and the operator relayed the message. He was tall and skinny, like Steve, and had big, gentle hands.

He took Killer inside and put him on a table, touching him carefully, examining him for broken bones, then reached for his stethoscope to listen to his heart and lungs.

"We tried to feed him," C.B. said, wiping her nose on her hand again. "Only he couldn't seem to swallow. Is his neck broken?"

The big fingers continued to probe. "No. But if he hung from a nail for a week, he's bound to have a pretty sore throat. His heart's good. Here, let's take off that collar." He unfastened it and handed it to me. "You kids go sit in the waiting room, OK? I'll see what I can do for him."

"Is he going to die?" I wanted to know.

"Not if I can help it. Killer's a pretty tough cat. If he can't eat right away, we'll get some nourishment into him through an IV. He's not too badly dehydrated, all things considered. I think he'll make it."

We sat in the waiting room, but Ben Newton said he had business to attend to; then he paused to look back at us from the doorway.

"Oh, maybe you'd like to know, Danny. We talked to Virgil Caspitorian. He admits he gave the key to the Holmans, insists it was for his aunts' own good. He didn't know the Holmans were making searches on their own, but *they* say the accidents were *his* idea. I expect we'll be bringing charges against both of them, although if they get good lawyers—which they will—we may not be able to pin anything on them. I don't think Miss Rosie and Miss Anna will have any more trouble with them, though."

"I'm glad of that," I said. I looked down at the collar in my hands, at the sparkling jewels set in the red leather. They looked just like the rhinestones in a necklace that Aunt Mattie wore to church sometimes.

"Sheriff," I said, "do you know how to tell if these are diamonds or junk?"

He looked startled. "Diamonds? In the cat's collar? Where'd you get such an idea as that?"

We told him, and Ben came back and took the collar and looked at it closely.

"Well, I haven't had much experience with diamonds," he said finally. "It seems to me, though, that these settings look different from the ones you usually find on a dog's collar. They have beveled edges around each stone, the way a gem in a ring has to keep it from coming loose, instead of prongs that might break off. All right with you if I take this along to Mr. Pritchard and see what he says?"

"Sure," I said, swallowing around the lump that wouldn't leave my throat. We couldn't hear a sound out of Killer in the next room, and I figured he must be in bad shape to let himself be handled without any protest at all.

"See you later," Ben told us and went back out to the patrol car.

C.B. looked up at the clock on the opposite wall. It was a quarter after five.

"I suppose it's too late now, even if Killer is OK, to take him out to the members of the Secret Club," she said.

I didn't say anything. I just sat and listened for some sound from the room where Dr. Baker was working over Killer, and Leroy rested his head against my knee while we waited.

"He'll have to stay here for a day or two," Dr. Baker said. "Or, rather, I'm going to take him home with me over the weekend. You can check back on Monday and see how he is. He doesn't seem to have any bones broken, and when he gets some fluids and some nourishment into him, I think he'll be all right. Once he starts eating on his own, I'll send him home."

We walked out into the late afternoon sunshine. We could see the blue of Indian Lake glistening through the trees. It was a lovely peaceful scene, one I'd come to enjoy in the short time I'd been here.

Only there wasn't any peace in my heart.

I started down the road, and C.B. caught hold of my sleeve. "Where are you going? It's almost suppertime."

"I don't care about supper. My throat feels about

like Killer's must feel. I'm going out to their Secret Club clubhouse. They're all still there."

She let go of my sweater but didn't move out of my way. "What are you going to say? What are you going to do?"

"I don't know," I said. "I'll know when I get there."

"Can I go with you?"

I only hesitated for a second. "All right. Come on."

We didn't talk all the way out there. We heard their voices before we got to the place where they were building the clubhouse and smelled the smoke of the fire they'd built on the beach for the hot dog roast.

I didn't realize, until we walked right into the middle of them, that the voices were angry. I guess I was too busy with my own thoughts, struggling to control the fury I felt. Even Leroy was subdued, sticking right at my side instead of rushing ahead the way he usually did.

Steve was the first one who saw us. He called out, "Danny!" and the others all fell silent.

I noticed that they were in a semicircle near the fire, facing Frankie. And Frankie looked angry—angry and maybe something else. Maybe frightened.

"What's going on?" C.B. muttered under breath.

They turned toward us, and for a few seconds nobody said anything.

Then Paul took a step toward us. "Did you find him, Danny? Did you find Killer?"

"We found him," I said and looked at Frankie.

"Where is he then?" Paul asked. Frankie didn't say anything; he was tense and wary, as if he expected someone to attack him.

"He's at Dr. Baker's," I said. "Did you hang him on that nail, Frankie? Are you really as rotten as that?"

There was an outraged, horrified murmuring

among the others. Even Frankie looked pale, and he licked his lips nervously.

"I don't know what you're talking about. I don't know anything about any nail," he said.

"We found him," I told him, "in the shed at your place. Hanging by his collar from a nail. He couldn't even swallow when we took him down. It's a wonder he was still alive. When did you put him there?"

"I didn't!" Frankie protested. "I never put him on any nail! I don't know anything about it!"

"You put him in the shed though, didn't you?" Steve asked. He turned his head to look at us, and he sounded angry. "We were just talking about it. Paul said it was about time Danny showed up with that cat, and Frankie laughed and said you wouldn't be coming so there was no point in waiting for you. He said it like a joke, only when we pinned him down he admitted he'd locked up the cat. As a joke, he said. He didn't say he'd done anything to hurt him."

"I didn't!" Frankie insisted. "I just threw the cage in the shed and left him there! I don't know anything about him being on a nail, for gosh sakes! Honest, I only shut him in the shed!"

The others were silent, their shock proving, if we needed proof, that it was only Frankie's idea, no one else's.

"The cage must have come open when I threw

it in there," Frankie said, nervous when nobody else said anything. "He got out when he came to and jumped around and got caught on the nail, if that's where you found him! You can't blame me for something I didn't know anything about!"

C.B. hadn't said anything up to then. "You never went back to check on him after you put him in there? Never took him any food or water?"

"It was only a few days," Frankie said. "Besides, there are mice in there. I figured he'd catch mice."

The silence stretched on and on while we all looked at him. Out on the lake a motor boat sounded like a mosquito in the distance until it faded off into more silence.

It was all I could do not to leap on Frankie, even if he was bigger than I was, and pound on him. I was the one who finally spoke.

"You said *when he came to.* How come he was unconscious when you put him in the cage?"

Frankie didn't answer that right away. It was finally getting through even Frankie's thick head that he was the only one who didn't think he'd done a terrible thing.

"Did you hurt him?" C.B. asked, and I could tell she wanted to hit him, too. Her hands were knotted into fists at her sides. "Did you hit him with something? Knock him out, so you could put him in the cage?"

Frankie tried to shrug it off. "I just tossed a rock at him. I didn't really expect to hit him. I didn't know it would knock him out."

Poor Killer, I thought. I didn't realize how much I'd admired that big, tough cat, until now. And it was my fault he'd been hurt and locked up. If I hadn't been trying to capture him, and Frankie wanting to keep me from doing it, none of it would have happened.

Steve dropped the stick he was holding into the fire, and it sent up a small shower of sparks. "You cheated, Frankie. In the worst way ever, you cheated. And even then Danny passed the initiation. He found Killer and caught him, before the deadline."

Frankie scowled. "He didn't bring him to us! That was part of it, he had to bring the cat to us!"

"But he was hurt! He had to take Killer to my dad!" Steve protested. "And if you hadn't had the cat locked up, Danny probably would have had him sooner. Danny's earned his way into the Secret Club, Frankie. I say he has. What do the rest of you guys says?"

There was a muttering around the circle. "Yeah." "Sure has." "He deserves to be in."

I drew in a deep breath. "You know something?" I said, and if my voice wasn't quite steady I hoped nobody but me would notice. "I think I earned my membership, too. But I don't want it any longer. I don't want to be part of your Secret Club. I don't want to be part of a gang that sets things for people to do that are hateful and hurting. Frankie didn't have the right to ask me to do anything to someone else's cat. Getting a bowling trophy out of a deserted cabin, the way Paul did, wasn't so bad. It didn't hurt anybody, although nobody really had a right to go into that cabin. But trying to capture Killer was a rotten thing, and I won't ever do anything like it again."

I glared defiantly at Frankie, who'd gotten his way after all. "Maybe I'll never have any friends in this town and I'll spend the whole year I'm here by myself or playing with girls. I'd rather do that than take a chance on getting to be like *Frankie*."

I was shaking, and I turned around and ran blindly through the woods, hardly able to see the path. I heard C.B. behind me, and we both had to stop and catch a breath when we got out to the road.

"Good for you," C.B. said. "I wish Sheriff Newton would put Frankie in jail for what he did."

I didn't want to talk about it. I really wanted to go off in the trees and be by myself, only I couldn't. It wasn't C.B.'s fault, and besides, she was the only friend I had in this goldanged town.

"Danny," C.B. said after a few minutes of silent walking. "Look!"

Reluctantly, I stopped and turned around.

And there they all came. Everybody but Frankie, even the kids I didn't know very well. They were all following us.

We just stood there until they caught up to us.

"We decided we didn't want to be part of the Secret Club any more, either," Paul said.

"We can make up another club," Steve added. "No reason it has to be a secret, or have initiations, either. Just a club to have fun."

Tubby, who was the last one to arrive, as he usually was, because he was too fat to walk very fast, gasped out, "We think you ought to be president of the new club, Danny. And think up a name for it. You're good at things like that."

This time the prickling in my eyes wasn't because I was angry. I couldn't say anything yet. I didn't know if I wanted to be president of a new club or not, and I wished more than ever that I could go off and be by myself. I sure didn't want anybody watching me to think I was *crying*.

"We didn't even get to eat our hot dogs," Tubby said. "And I left my potato chips back there on the beach."

Paul snickered. "Maybe it will do you good, Tubby," he said. "To miss a meal." He sobered. "And maybe it will do Frankie good, too, to eat by himself. If he feels like eating now."

"It makes me sick," Steve said, "to think of him treating a cat that way."

There was a muttering of agreement, and then another kid spoke up. I knew his name, Randy Stocum. He was a little, skinny kid with thick glasses, and he was practically a genius in math.

"I'm sorry about the cat, but I'm glad this happened. You know why? Because I've been disliking some of the things Frankie did, and I've been afraid to say so. Once I disagreed with him and he threatened to break my glasses. And I was afraid not to go along with everyone else when Frankie said he was running for president of the club."

"Me, too," someone else said, and a louder voice chimed in, "Frankie's always pushed everybody around. But if we all quit knuckling under to him at once, what can he do?"

"If I'm not going to get the hot dogs," Tubby said, "I have to hurry up and get home before they finish supper."

Everybody laughed, then. It was a relief to laugh when I'd felt like crying.

"Hey, Danny," Steve said, "I'll call you tomorrow and let you know how Killer's doing, OK?"

"Thanks. I'd appreciate it," I told him.

Everybody scattered, heading for home. We were going to be late, but I figured Gramps and Aunt Mattie would understand.

When we walked past the sheriff's office, we could see Ben Newton inside at his desk, doing his paperwork. I knew he hated that part of being a police officer, making out all those reports and things. We didn't intend to stop, but he looked up and saw us and waved us in. He got up and started pushing things around on his cluttered desk.

"Come on in. I've got something for you," he said. "If I can find it in all this mess. Ah, here they are!"

He came around the desk carrying something in his hand, and when he was right in front of us, I saw what it was. A badge—or, rather, two badges. They looked just like his, except that they said *Deputy* instead of *Sheriff*.

"Here," he said. "Pin these on yourselves. I don't know how I solved any crimes around here before you showed up. You deserve these."

C.B. looked at him incredulously. "Are they real?"

"Well, I picked 'em up over at the dime store. The county's a bit picky about what they'll pay for, so I bought 'em myself. But I have the authority to swear in deputies, and I'm swearing you in."

We both opened our mouths to remind him that he'd sworn us in, and Paul, too, the night we caught the men who kidnapped Mrs. Trentwood's dog, but he flapped a hand to shush us up.

"I know, I know. You've already taken the oath. Here's the proof you're really deputies, though.

There's only one thing. You have to promise me that you won't get involved in any more mysteries until I get caught up on the paperwork for the ones I already have. Agreed?"

It was a joke, then. I didn't think it was terribly funny, and C.B. wasn't laughing, either. But Ben Newton thought it was hilarious. He was laughing in the way people have when they're really satisfied with themselves.

"Oh, by the way," he said, when we had turned to go, "you're pretty good detectives, for real. The stones in Killer's collar *are* diamonds. Mr. Pritchard nearly had heart failure when he realized those valuable gems had been riding around a cat's neck for heaven knows how long. One of the other cats also has a collar with real jewels—or, I should say, she did have. I talked the old ladies into taking it off, and we're discussing a safer place to keep them. They figured nobody would think they were anything but rhinestones, and that way Virgil wouldn't ever get his hands on them." He shook his head, amusement gone.

"It's a miracle they didn't lose the whole batch. Amazing, what people will do! Anyway, while I was talking to them, I told them you'd found their cat, and that he was at the veterinarian's. I wouldn't be surprised but what they're cooking up some kind of reward for you, for saving both the cat and the collar."

"I don't want any reward," I said, feeling uncomfortable, remembering how much of the whole thing was my fault.

"Well, now, don't be so selfish that you deprive those old ladies of the pleasure of giving you a reward," Ben said. "And remember, you're entitled to those badges only if you follow orders. No more mysteries for at least a month."

We left him laughing to himself as he shuffled his papers.

"Grown-ups are weird," C.B. said. She had pinned the badge to the front of her sweater. "Imagine, we're really deputies!"

"Yeah. Until we try to *be* deputies. He just has a funny way of telling us to mind our own business and stay out of trouble."

"I suppose. The badges are sort of neat, though." She polished it with her hand.

Ahead of us, Leroy suddenly froze, peering into the alley.

"What's the matter with Leroy?"

"Maybe he sees some bank robbers," I said. "Or kidnappers. Or someone's trying to break into the back door of the pharmacy."

The hair was bristling on the back of Leroy's neck, and he growled. I put a hand on his collar. "Come on. We're going to mind our own business, remember? No more Minden Curse, not for a whole month."

C.B.'s face was serious. "I can't see anything wrong back there, just a couple of guys standing there talking. You suppose they're plotting something illegal?"

"How would Leroy know that?" I asked, tugging on his collar.

"I don't know either of them. Do you?" C.B. had stopped and was staring openly at the two men beside the garbage cans in the alley. "Maybe we ought to tell the sheriff about them, so he can check on them."

"What, and have him take our new badges away?" I demanded. "Nothing doing." I gave a hard jerk on Leroy and dragged him away. "Come on, let's go! I'm as bad as Tubby, I'm getting *hungry!*"

I suddenly felt great. The Holmans and Virgil were no longer a danger to the Cat Ladies. The old sisters had enough money to fix their roof, and their fortune would no longer be left on cat collars where something could happen to it. And Killer was safe and would be getting better. I wondered if I could really make friends with Killer, when his throat wasn't sore any more, so he could eat the liver I'd bring him.

C.B. looked at me and grinned.

"OK, deputy," she said. "I'll race you to the corner."

I let go of Leroy's collar and we ran, Leroy ahead of us with his ears flapping and his tongue hanging out.

"Hey," I called to C.B., "Ben forgot something! He should have had a badge for Leroy, too!"

"Next time we see him, let's ask for one!" C.B. said, and we were both laughing like crazy when we got to the corner.

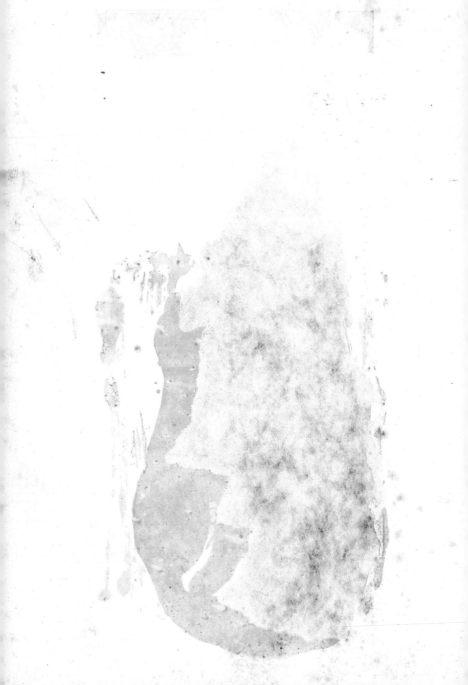